MW01596564

Know Me, Cowboy

Honeywood Ranch Book 2

WILLOW WHITE

NEW CREATION PUBLISHING

KNOW ME, COWBOY. Copyright © 2023 by Willow White. All rights reserved.

This novel is a work of fiction. Names, characters, businesses, organizations, places, events, and incidents are either the products of the author's imagination or used in a fictitious manner.

Chapter 1

Something was wrong with the lights. *Thank God I'm wearing my straw hat, or I'd be blind.* Mindy flashed a dazzling smile and launched into the chorus with gusto as beads of sweat broke out on her forehead. She looked at the women and girls pressed against the stage, singing along. They knew every word. Mindy's vision blurred. Something wasn't right. Why was it so hot? Why were those lights so *bright?*

Why was this dress so tight? She kept singing, reaching up to loosen her collar—but she wasn't wearing one. Of course she wasn't wearing a collar. Like they'd let her wear a collar. She stopped dancing, stopped moving, and kept singing, trying to breathe between the lyrics, but she couldn't get any air into her lungs.

She stepped back from the lights. *Just breathe. Relax. You're almost done.* But she couldn't breathe, and she couldn't relax.

Why weren't those women singing anymore? Or smiling? One of the women looked so much like a mom, and she wore a mom's concern on her face.

Mindy realized she'd stopped singing. She tried to smile, but it was a lot of work. Her face muscles tried to obey her, but they couldn't quite manage it. She spun away from the crowd, but the concern etched on her drummer's face told her that she was in trouble. She brought the mic up to her mouth to say something witty; she was always quick on her feet, but no words came out. She dropped the mic, and the *bang* shot out of the speakers.

This dress was too tight. She hated this dress so much. She hated every thread of it—though there weren't many. If she hadn't been standing in front of a thousand adoring fans, she would've ripped it off. She gasped for air, bending over to rest her hands on her knees. Her lungs burned. One by one her band members stopped playing. This was really happening. What a nightmare. Her lead guitar approached. "Here, let's sit down—"

She shook off his helping hand. "I'm fine," she croaked.

In the distance a man shouted at the crowd to let him through.

"I'm fine!" she said, a little louder. "It's just a ... a ..." She didn't know what it was. She looked up and saw gray uniforms working their way toward her. EMTs. Cops too. She looked around wildly. This wasn't supposed to happen. She had to get out of here. She looked at the crowd. They were shoulder to shoulder. She'd never get through there. She turned around.

Backstage. If she could get there, she could keep going. There was no one back there. But there was equipment—lots of it—blocking her path. It wasn't piled up very high. She could jump over it, but if that curtain didn't give way, she didn't know what would happen.

Think. She couldn't think. All she could do was feel.

And all she could feel was fear.

She tried to suck in a lungful, managed to get some air into her lungs, and pushed off. This was going to kill her, she thought, as she pumped her arms. Like running through molasses. *Breathe in. Breathe out. Run.*

The stage was too cramped for much of a running start, but she drove her boots into the stage, gaining speed. Her vision blurred again, and she couldn't judge the distance to that equipment. She pushed off like she was in a long jump championship. What she really needed right now was a pole vault. Her cowboy boots sailed over the equipment, and she brought her arms up to deal with the curtain, which gave way like air.

Finally, something had gone her way.

She already felt free, and she'd only gone forty feet. Her boots crashed down too early—the ramp. She'd forgotten the stupid ramp was there. Pain shot up her leg, but she kept going. Shouting followed her, but she didn't hear any footfall. She ran, focusing most of her effort into forcing air into her burning lungs—it was like trying to suck a Frosty through a straw.

Her feet pounded down the historic Main Street of Deadwood. She had to get off Main Street. There, on the right. Gold Street. She could turn there. She didn't know where Gold Street led, but it had to be better than Main Street.

There weren't many people on the street in this part of town. Most of the festival was behind her. But still flashes went off as phones captured her ridiculous getaway sprint. She turned right onto Gold Street and stuttered to a panicked stop. It was clogged with picnic tables full of people. She looked behind her and saw people chasing. She looked at Gold Street again, and her vision blurred all of those people into one solid mass.

"Here!" someone shouted from ahead.

She couldn't see the person, but she started that way.

"Here!" she heard again. "Over here!"

She felt like she was dying. Maybe she should just stop. *No. Keep going.*

The crowd split to make a hole for her, and she picked up speed, until a woman in a bra and underwear jumped out in front of her, shouting, "Here!"

She stopped again, her momentum nearly carrying her forward into the half-naked woman's arms.

"Here!" She thrust a wad of fabric into Mindy's arms. "Give me your hat!" She plucked the hat off Mindy's head and stabbed it onto her own. "Now, go!" She was already pulling on a sweatshirt to go with her new hat. Mindy didn't understand, but she kept moving. She was too tired to run, but she quickly walked to the end of the street and turned left in the alley. She ducked behind a dumpster and tried to catch her breath, while she looked down at whatever had been shoved into her hands.

It was a dress.

The alley did not provide enough light to give much more information than that. She heard footsteps and male voices, so, hugging the wall and its handy shadows, she slid down the alley.

The voices were gaining on her. She heard her name, and she heard anger, which sparked her adrenaline, which made her aware of two new pieces of information: one, at some point in the last few minutes, her breathing had mostly returned to normal; and two, she was staring at a parking garage.

She darted across the alley and climbed headfirst through a glassless window. It was a good thing she worked out so often, or this would have been much more complicated.

She landed inside the garage and looked up to see a spattering of people. All staring at her. Mindy smiled, trying to act natural, and then remembered that she was wearing a slinky dress covered in rhinestones.

And now she knew why that woman had handed her a dress. She quickly threw it on over her head and walked to her left with purpose, as if she had somewhere important to be. She heard one of those rubberneckers say her name and "west end of parking garage."

Seriously? Was she going to come this far only to get caught in a parking garage wearing two dresses? She looked around for a hiding spot. There wasn't one, but she was inches away from a pickup that read West Hope Water District on the side. She had no idea where West Hope was, but she took the word *hope* as a sign from the Almighty, and she put one foot on the top of a rear tire and then gracefully leapt into the bed of the truck.

She lay down and listened.

It felt *so* good to lie down. It felt *so* good to hold still.

She didn't hear anything for a while, but then one of her roadies said, "They said she went this way."

A voice she didn't recognize said, "But she's obviously not here."

She held her breath. It would be so embarrassing to get caught hiding in the back of a pickup in the Deadwood parking garage. Wearing two dresses.

They argued some more, and then their voices grew faint.

She had escaped them, but now what was she going to do? She didn't have any money on her. She didn't have her ID. She didn't have her phone.

All she had were two dresses: city girl dress and country girl dress. And the rhinestones on the city girl dress were really starting to chafe.

She started to sit up, but then she heard singing. Really, really bad singing. She lay back down and waited for it to pass.

Chapter 2

Dustin Honeywood pulled his pickup out of the Deadwood garage and promptly got stuck in traffic. There seemed to be a mad rush to get out of town, which was weird because the Mindy Rose concert had only just started.

She'd probably started singing that terrible song "Flirt till Flirty Fails" and sent them running for the hills. He was painfully sick of that song, but he also knew that most people loved it. That's why the radio station played it to death.

He rolled down his window and didn't hear any music coming from the stage in the middle of Main Street. And he hadn't realized it at the time, but he hadn't heard any on his way to the truck either. That was weird. Maybe the concert had been canceled? Was there a threat of rain? He stuck his head out to get a good look at the sky—and only saw stars. Clear as clean glass.

He started to roll the window back up but then changed his mind. The fresh air felt good. Dustin was almost always in a good mood, but tonight, he was even happier than usual. He'd sung a new song at an open mic, and he'd gotten lots of positive feedback. Now he was high on life. He hit shuffle on his classic country playlist and then when John Anderson started singin' about swingin', Dustin sang along—with zeal.

He sang all the way out of downtown Deadwood, and then he sang his way onto 14A. He took a short break from singing for a Dolly Parton song—though he was his only audience right now, even he didn't want to listen to himself singing soprano—but when her song gave way to "Baby's Got Her Blue Jeans On," he picked back up and sang himself all the way back to West Hope.

Dustin's house was currently being fumigated for termites, so he was staying at the Honeywood Ranch, which two of his five brothers owned. He was grateful that they were so hospitable. He could afford to stay at a hotel, but he never slept well in hotels.

When he pulled into his brothers' driveway, he transitioned from singing to humming. He knew he didn't have a good voice and didn't want to hear Chase's commentary on his lack of ability.

He grabbed his guitar case, got out of the truck, swung the door shut, and started toward the front door. Then he remembered that he'd left his lunch cooler in the back of the truck and turned back to get it. He reached over the rail and into the bed of his truck, and when his fingers grabbed soft, warm flesh, he screamed like a little girl.

Chapter 3

M indy sat bolt upright in the truck and begged this strange man to stop screaming.

He did so promptly, and then he held perfectly still, as if he'd been unplugged.

A porch light lit the yard behind him, so it was impossible to make out any of his features. Was he old? Young? His scream had made him sound young. And also, unhinged.

The silence was vast. Why wasn't he saying anything? Was he waiting for her to say something? She had no idea what to say. Thank you for the ride? Sorry about stowing away in your truck? Where are we? She could see no other buildings beyond this property. A ranch house and two barns. Probably. It was hard to see anything past the porch light.

She needed a phone. Her mother was going to panic if she heard about this from anyone other than Mindy herself. She opened her mouth to ask for his cell, but he chose that moment to say, "Why are you in my truck?"

Something about the matter-of-fact way that he said it made her laugh. Also, she noted that the porch light was shining directly at her like a spotlight, and he'd done nothing to suggest that he recognized her.

Given the age of the songs he'd chosen to belt out all the way home, in the wrong key, and once with the wrong lyrics—he'd somehow turned Nitty Gritty's "lazy yellow moon" into a mangled southern accent version of "Louisiana moon"—there was a chance that he didn't know who she was. There was a chance that he hadn't heard a country song released since 1987.

Maybe he wasn't as young as his girly little scream had suggested.

"I'm sorry," she said. "I needed a place to hide. When you drove off, I didn't know what to do." She laughed uneasily. "I've sort of been panicking the whole way here."

"You're lucky I'm not a serial killer."

Well, *that* was a creepy thing to say. "Yeah, I guess so. Could I, uh, use your phone?

"Yeah, of course." He whipped it out and handed it to her. "You were hiding from someone?" He glanced toward the road. "Are you in danger?"

She saw the time on his phone, and her heart sank. It was way too late to call her mother. She needed to call Keely, her best friend back home. Keely was the only one she could really trust. Keely wouldn't rat her out to her manager or to a blogger or to anyone else, and Keeley would come get her. But Keely lived in Alabama. A fat load of good Keely's willingness to act as chauffeur was going to do her when she was stranded in the middle of the Great Plains. And she was ashamed to realize she didn't have Keely's phone number memorized. She had it plugged into her phone, of course, but she didn't have her phone. She would have to call Keely's parents, who still had a land line, and she wasn't going to do that tonight. She handed him his phone back. "You know what? I don't remember my friend's number. Uh ..." She had no idea what to say. She couldn't exactly ask this guy for a ride back into town.

Maybe she needed to call her manager. Maybe the jig was up.

At the front of the house another light popped on. "Everything okay?" a man called out.

Did this guy live with his dad? Had she stowed away in some teenager's truck? The gossip rag potential of this story just kept getting better and better.

"Yeah, yeah," he called back. "Be right in."

With the extra light she could read the sign beside the driveway: Honeywood Ranch: Event Center, and then in smaller words beneath: weddings, reunions, retreats, and more.

"Your dad owns an event center?"

He laughed dryly. "So many things wrong with that guess."

"What does that mean?"

"He's not my dad. He's my brother, and I don't live here. And he's sort of trying to have an event center, but there are no events here, so no, really, he is just the owner of an expensive sign."

"Oh." That was a lot of information. "But you have like rooms here?"

"Who are you hiding from?"

"Okay, so I'm sorry that I hid in your truck, but the truth is, I have a friend I can call. I just know that I can't get a ride till tomorrow. I can't pay you right now, but I promise to pay you when she gets here. Could I just crash in one of your rooms?" She could feel his resistance. "I'll pay double."

"I don't know if the rooms are ready," he said slowly.

No wonder they hadn't had any events yet.

"And it's not really my call. If you would just tell me who you're hiding from, I would probably be more inclined toward hospitality."

So he screamed like a little kid, but talked like an old man and listened to old man music. She wanted so bad to ask him how old he was, but he was waiting for an answer.

She scrambled to come up with a lie. She was a terrible liar, always had been. It was one of the reasons she was struggling with her music career. She was living a lie. She took a big breath. "I was at Wild Bill Days, and ..." She remembered a movie she'd watched recently and had an idea. "And I met some friends there, but I didn't really know them, and they started acting really weird, and I got scared that they were going to do something to me."

He woke up his phone screen. "What are their names? I'll call the sheriff."

"No!" She reached out and laid her hand over the phone, accidentally touching his hand. She jerked her hand back. "Sorry."

"Why are you saying no?"

What was she supposed to say? They hadn't called the sheriff in the movies. This guy had gone off script.

The door to the house opened again. "Are you sure everything's all right?"

He held out his hand. "Come on. Let's go meet Hudson before *he* calls the sheriff."

She took his warm hand, and though she didn't need his help climbing out of the truck, she accepted it. Suddenly, she was very tired. Physically exhausted and emotionally depleted.

She fell into step beside him as he walked toward the light. It was pretty weird that this guy hadn't recognized her. What were the chances she was going to get past his brother as well? Not very good. This whole charade was not going to last much longer.

She couldn't imagine what she looked like, and she tried to smooth out her hair as they went up the front steps. Her new friend opened the door for her, and when she looked up to thank him, she nearly staggered backward.

Holy jumpin' hot beans.

This guy was not old. He was not young either. She was Goldilocks, and he was just right. He was the most gorgeous thing she'd seen this side of the Mississippi.

"Are you okay?"

"Yeah, uh, just a little rattled, I think."

He nodded. "Understandable. You've had quite a night."

He had no idea. But right now, this close, this porch light was incredibly bright. She wasn't hiding anything. She was completely exposed. And she didn't see so much as a flicker of recognition on his face.

He opened the door, and she stepped inside to see a living room *full* of people.

Oh no.

Chapter 4

Dustin waited for someone to say something stupid, but no one did. They all just stared at his gorgeous stowaway. He cleared his throat and pointed at Hudson. "This is my oldest brother, Hudson. He and Chase own this place." He pointed at Chase. "That's Chase." The look on Chase's face was completely incredulous. It almost made Dustin laugh. "And that's my brother Wyatt and his girlfriend Olivia."

Olivia made a beeline for them, extending her hand. "Hi! Welcome!"

"And this is—" He gestured to her, inviting her to introduce herself.

She hesitated as if she couldn't remember her name and then almost shouted, "Mandy! Mandy ... Violet."

He stared at her, unsure of how to respond to that outburst.

"Welcome to Honeywood Ranch," Olivia said. "Come on in and have a seat. Tell us about yourself."

"Uh, actually." Dustin snagged the newcomer's hand to keep her from getting sucked into the vortex. "She was just wondering if she could crash here. She's uh ..." He wasn't sure how to put this. "She's had a pretty crazy night, and she lost her phone. She can call a friend in the morning, but ..."

"So this is a thing now?" Chase grumbled. "Gorgeous women going to keep getting stranded on our ranch?" He shook his head and got up from his chair, no doubt to go hide from the swelling crowd.

"Of course she can stay!" Olivia declared after a weird silence. She snatched their guest's free hand and pulled her away from Dustin. "I'll show you to the guest room." She dragged her away.

Dustin looked at Hudson to make sure it was okay. It wasn't really up to Olivia. It was clear that Hudson didn't mind.

Wyatt came toward him, his brow furrowed. "Uh ... isn't that—"

Dustin shushed him. "Yes, yes it is. But obviously she doesn't want us to know that."

"Why not?"

"I don't know. She was supposed to be headlining in Deadwood tonight. I think something bad might have happened. She's pretty shook up. I figured she'd tell me when she was ready." He looked at his brother. "She's not ready."

Wyatt nodded. "Okay, man. It's your barbecue. Honey?" he called out to Olivia. "Are you ready to go?"

Olivia came out of the guest room. "I'm just going to heat her up some leftover supper real quick."

Wyatt groaned and went back into the living room. "Guess I might as well sit for a few more minutes, then."

Dustin joined him.

"So how did this happen?" Hudson asked him.

Dustin didn't really want to tell him. "I'm not really sure. She needed help, so I helped. But I don't know what happened to make her need that help."

Hudson frowned. "Why are you speaking in riddles? You must have some idea."

Dustin sighed. "I do, but I'm trying to respect her privacy. I don't know how much she wants us to know. She was in a hurry to get out of Deadwood." *Is it a lie if you recycle her lie?* "She said something about friends acting weird and that she got spooked. So her friend is coming to rescue her, but that friend can't get here till tomorrow."

"Should we call the sheriff?" Hudson asked.

Dustin shook his head. "She doesn't want to involve the law."

Hudson raised an eyebrow. "Is she a criminal? Did you bring us a fugitive, little brother?" He laughed, but Dustin didn't know if he was joking or if he was legitimately concerned. "Mandy Violet ..." he said thoughtfully. "Sounds like an alias to me."

Wyatt and Dustin exchanged a look.

"I don't think she's a criminal," Dustin said. "She seems nice."

"You mean that she seems beautiful," Hudson said.

"Yeah, that too."

"And she just took your guest room," Hudson said.

Dustin chuckled. "Yep. That's okay. Olivia gave it to her, and we all know that Olivia is in charge."

Wyatt laughed. "Stop it."

"I'm just kidding," Dustin said. He liked Olivia. He liked how happy she made his brother.

"Mandy Violet," Hudson said again. "Maybe we should look her up online."

Dustin suppressed a groan.

"I'll do it." Wyatt whipped out his phone and then long before he could have possibly done a thorough search said, "I'm not seeing anything."

"Nothing?" Hudson said. "Not even any social media?"

Clearly annoyed, Wyatt said no and tucked his phone back into his pocket.

"Huh," Hudson said. "I really don't think that's her name, then."

It was a good thing she hadn't said much since coming into the house. Her southern accent was as thick as grits and would have made Hudson even more curious. He would have asked her where she was from, and she would have lied again, and she was a *terrible* liar. This made him like her. *Nope.* Probably shouldn't go forming a crush on Mindy Rose, no matter how beautiful she was. "Well, if she robs us or kills us in our sleep, you can blame me."

Hudson laughed. "Okay, deal."

Chapter 5

"This is delicious." Mindy hadn't realized how hungry she was. How could shepherd's pie taste this good? Granted, it had bacon in it, but still. It wasn't anything fancy. Of course, she hadn't eaten anything in days, and she hadn't had any real, home-cooked food in weeks. "Did you make this?" she asked with her mouth full.

Olivia smiled proudly. "I did. You want to know the secret?"

She didn't really have a way to put such a secret to use, but she didn't want to offend her. "Sure."

She leaned closer. "Turnips."

What? *Turnips?*

Olivia nodded proudly. "You mash a little turnip into the potato. It gives it that *zip!*" She said the word *zip* with great excitement. This woman was passionate about her root vegetables.

Mindy looked around the room. "So, this is it? They let the guests stay in their house?"

Olivia laughed. "Oh no. They're putting some rooms in the barn. This is their actual guest room."

"Oh. Well, it's nice of them to let me crash here. I really will try to get out of their hair in the morning."

"The Honeywoods are a very hospitable bunch. Trust me. You're not the first person to crash here." She giggled. "And you didn't exactly *crash*."

Mindy didn't get the joke. "Yeah, wow. Four brothers, huh?"

"Six, actually. Seth is the baby of the family, and he's not here. And Burke is at a rodeo. I think. That's usually the answer I get when I ask where he is, anyway."

Wow, *six* brothers. Her eyelids felt like her eyelashes were wearing weights. She set the bowl on her nightstand, and Olivia promptly grabbed it. "Can I get you anything else? Water? Tea? Hudson has lots of good herbal teas, good for helping you sleep."

"I don't think I'll have any trouble sleeping, but thank you."

"You're very welcome. Okay, I'm going to be getting home, but if you need anything, Hudson is super helpful. He's a doctor. Chase, the other one who lives here, he can be a bit grumpy, but don't let him fool you. He's got a gentle heart of gold."

Mindy nodded, a little overwhelmed by all the insight. "Thank you."

"You betcha. Sleep tight!" She pulled the door shut behind her. Mindy got up and walked to the mirror to see how bad the damage was.

She nearly gasped at the sight of the pretty purple dress she wore. It fit her perfectly, accentuating her waist in a flattering way. She couldn't see any evidence of the hideous dress that hid beneath it. When this was all over, she was going to make a sincere effort to find that crazy woman on Gold Street and thank her appropriately. What a hero.

She pulled the pretty dress off over her head and then grimaced when she saw what lay underneath. She hurriedly peeled that one off her body, threw it into the corner, and then realized how bad of an idea that was. She scooped it up and looked around for a trash can.

She found one in the bathroom. She shoved the dress down into the small rubbage bin and then balled up a bunch of toilet paper and put it on top. Not that these people were going to go through her trash, but, well, people had gone through her trash before.

She went back into the bedroom, put the purple cotton dress back on, and then slid beneath the covers. Wow, what an incredibly comfortable bed.

What incredibly friendly people. She really liked Olivia. What a nice woman. She reminded her of Keely. Mindy couldn't remember the last time she'd made a new friend. Every "friend" she made now was always after something, always had some agenda. But Olivia hadn't even recognized her. She'd been that friendly just for the sake of it. How refreshing. Maybe Mindy could have two friends in this world.

And on that happy thought, the country music sensation Mindy Rose drifted off to a dreamless sleep.

Chapter 6

Dustin didn't know that Wyatt was following him outside until he was on the steps and realized he wasn't alone. He looked at him expectantly. "What?"

"Where are you going?"

"Nowhere. Just trying to avoid Hudson's curiosity."

Wyatt chuckled. "Can't blame you there."

"Thought I'd get some fresh air."

"Olivia will figure out who she is," Wyatt said, "if she hasn't already. She likes country, and she's not stupid."

Dustin sighed. "I figured. But I think our secret star will vanish in the morning." The thought made him sad. Mindy was obviously unhappy. He wished he could help her. But her problems were probably way above his pay grade. Or even his ability to understand.

"So until then, we're just supposed to pretend we don't recognize her?"

Dustin laughed. "Will you relax? Are you and Olivia spending the night here?"

"No, but I'm going to drive her home, and I'm guessing Miss Mandy Violet will come up in conversation."

Dustin shrugged. "I'm not in charge here. You do what you need to do, I guess. But that woman literally ran away from her stage, from her tour, from her people, from her *fans*. And then she *hid* in the back of my truck. These are the actions of a desperate woman." *Or a completely crazy one,* he silently added. But he didn't think she was crazy. "And then she lied about her name, so she obviously wants to keep hiding."

"Well, let's hope that she doesn't jump into the shower and burst out in song."

"I very much doubt that she will sing in the shower. And if she does, it will only be the three of us to hear her. I already know her secret identity, Hudson won't know any better because he only listens to that weird instrumental stuff, and Chase will be out with the horses."

The screen door banged shut as Olivia came outside. Wyatt turned around to greet her. "Ready to go, hon?"

"Yes." Olivia stopped in front of Dustin. "Do you know anything about this girl?"

Oh no. "Why?"

"Because I'm worried about her. She just attacked her leftovers like she hadn't eaten in weeks, and she looks awful skinny."

"Maybe you're just that good of a cook."

She didn't laugh. "I'm serious. I don't know what kind of a weekend she's having, but I don't think she's okay. Just ... just protect yourself, okay?" She looped her arm through Wyatt's. "I know it worked out well for Wyatt to take in a stray, but sometimes stray animals bite."

Dustin didn't like that comment one bit. And it seemed out of character for Olivia.

"I'm not trying to be judgmental," she hurried to say. "I'm just feeling protective of you. And that accent? Where on earth is she from, the deep south?"

Yep. That's exactly where she was from, but he didn't see how that made her any more dangerous. "You guys have a safe drive home."

Wyatt looked annoyed with both of them. "Let me know if you need anything," he said to Dustin and then gently tugged Olivia toward his truck.

Olivia allowed herself to be pulled, though it was obvious she wasn't quite ready. "You make sure she gets a good breakfast."

Dustin rolled his eyes in the dark. "I will." The woman was rich and famous. He didn't know what problems she had, and he didn't doubt they were big, but he doubted that one of them was starvation.

He watched Wyatt's taillights fade into the night. Then he sat down and stared out into the darkness for a while. He had to wait for Hudson to go to bed so that he could take the couch.

He'd sure picked a fine time to have a termite problem.

Chapter 7

M indy woke up and reached toward the nightstand for her phone. When her hand didn't land on it, she groggily groped around, knocking something off in the process. When she heard it *thud* on the hardwood, she remembered where she was, and the insane events of the night before came flooding back in a painful deluge.

She had really done it. It reminded her of when she was in junior high. She'd been too proud to plug her nose before jumping into the pool, so over and over she'd gotten water up her nose. Oh how it had burned her nose and throat, making her eyes water. That's what she'd done last night—jumped into the deep end and sucked a bunch of chlorine up her nose.

She sat up and looked down at the spilled tea. Olivia had sneaked it into her room after she'd already gotten in bed, saying, "I just couldn't leave for the night thinking that you might get thirsty." What a weird and wonderful human that woman was. *But you'll probably never see her again.* This thought made her a lot sadder than seemed reasonable.

She went to the bathroom and brought a towel back to sop up the mess. Only then did she scan the room for a clock. She gasped.

She'd slept past noon! How was that even possible? She held her breath and listened, but she couldn't hear any sounds of life. She reached for the doorknob and then thought better of it. Maybe she should glance in a mirror first. She might step out of the room into a crowd of paparazzi. She knew this wouldn't happen. They were rarely stealthy and never quiet, but still ... She looked in the mirror and nearly cried out. Her eye makeup had devolved into two rings of black soot; her hair looked like a family of mice had moved in; and the glitter that had once been on her eyelids had somehow magically traveled all over her face. She glanced back at the pillowcase. Sure enough, there was plenty of glitter there too.

She went back into the bathroom and did the best she could with her limited supplies. Then she straightened her clothing and took a deep breath.

There was no one in the kitchen. Or the living room. She looked outside and didn't see anyone. A truck sat in the driveway, but it wasn't a water district truck.

They had left her alone. She admired their small-town trust. She looked around for a phone. She really needed to call her mother. She couldn't believe she'd slept that late.

The corner of their living room doubled as a small office, and a phone sat on the desk. She called her mom first, who, thank God, hadn't yet heard any news. "I wanted to warn you because I know they're going to make a big deal of it," she said slowly, "but it's not a big deal. I just needed a break."

She was slow to respond. "Are you sure you are okay? Won't you get into trouble?"

"Maybe." She sighed. "I don't plan to, though. I'm sorry, Mom. I didn't mean to be dramatic. I just sort of ... had a ... meltdown. I was overtired and overworked and ..." She didn't really understand what had happened, only that the pressure had built to the blowing up point, but she didn't know how to explain that to her mother. She didn't want to sound like she was complaining about a completely blessed career that allowed her to have everything she needed and wanted—well, almost everything. The autonomy and peace of mind were sorely lacking. "Anyway, I think Vern might call you, but please don't tell him where I am."

"Vern," she said slowly.

"My manager."

"I know that."

"Sorry. Just please don't tell anyone anything, but I wanted you to know that I'm fine. I'll figure this out. But don't call my phone. I don't have it."

"You ran off without your phone?"

She opened her mouth to defend herself. She didn't like the phrase *ran off*, but that's exactly what she'd done. Literally. She'd run. As fast as she could down Main Street in a spandex dress. It was a good thing she'd been wearing cowboy boots, not those awful strappy stilettos they sometimes forced onto her feet. She couldn't even imagine what she had looked like sprinting like that, but she knew she'd find out. There would definitely be pictures. She exhaled slowly. "Yes, Mom. I ran off without my phone. But I'll either get it back or get a new one soon."

"How am I supposed to reach you in the meantime?"

Mindy would have been annoyed, but her mom sounded scared. "You know what? I'm going to call Keely right now and ask her to come get me. And I'll head home to see you, okay?"

"Okay. I always liked that Keely."

"I know you did, Mom. I always liked her too. I love you, Mom. I'll call again soon, okay? In the meantime, please don't worry."

"I'll try not to."

Mindy said goodbye and hung up. She felt someone standing behind her and whirled around to find one of the brothers.

"Sorry, I didn't mean to startle you."

"No, it's okay. It's your house. At least I think it is? I got a little confused last night with who was who."

"Yeah. It's my house. Sort of."

She didn't know what that meant. She stood up. "Well, thanks for letting me use your phone, even though I didn't ask permission first." She smiled uneasily. "Where is everyone else?"

"Church."

Oh. "You don't go to church?"

"I do sometimes, but I didn't want to leave you here alone."

At first she thought that was a sweet sentiment, but then she inferred that he didn't trust her. "Oh."

He exhaled slowly, puffing his cheeks out. "I hope I don't regret asking this, but are you okay? I mean, not superficially. I don't really care about that. I just get the sense that you've got some chaos going on inside." He spoke slowly, thoughtfully, carefully. "And I know a little about chaos, so ..."

She didn't know what he was offering, exactly, but his intention was pure. "You're right about the chaos, but I really think I'm going to be okay. Thank you, though."

He nodded. "Okay, good." Then he turned and went out the front door.

What an interesting man. And it seemed he didn't recognize her either. Did she really look that different without all the airbrushing? Maybe. Or maybe none of these people listened to country music. She didn't think that was likely on a ranch in South Dakota, but she'd recently learned to never say never.

She heard engines and then tires on dirt. It seemed the churchgoers had returned, and she hadn't even called Keely yet. Shoot.

Chapter 8

D ustin had spent the entire sermon playing on his phone. He hadn't meant to, but once he started down the Mindy Rose rabbit hole, it was hard to get back out.

He'd expected there would already be some info out there about what had happened at the concert, but he was still disappointed to see it. He didn't know what was going on with Mindy, but he imagined it was pretty stressful to have absolutely no privacy. Several online magazines already had articles. The titles were hooky and promised to explain what had happened, but the actual articles offered almost no information. And each of them said the same thing, like they'd all cut and pasted from the same source: Mindy Rose abruptly stopped singing, ran and jumped off the back of the stage, and then disappeared.

He knew more information than any of these so-called reporters.

A light bulb went off in his head. So *that* was why she hadn't revealed her identity. He was trying to make her motivations big and complicated, but they weren't. She probably thought that he would simply call one of these stupid publications and give them the scoop.

Of course, he wouldn't have done that, but she didn't know that. She didn't know anything about him. And for that matter, he didn't know anything about her, either. Sure, he knew the words to all her hit songs, but so did thousands of other people. He wondered if she wrote her own songs, and he searched for their lyrics to find out.

Nope, he couldn't find a single song that she had written. No big deal. Lots of artists weren't songwriters. She didn't need to be a song-writer. She had a voice that could carry her career. But he was still a little disappointed. If she had written some songs, then he could have gone back over those lyrics and tried to learn a little about her. While he appreciated her talent, he'd never really been her biggest fan. He didn't want to be judgmental, but her songs could be a bit ... trashy. And he was more into older country, anyway.

He did another search for her name, and this time he added "Wild Bill Days" to the search. This returned dozens and dozens of results. He clicked on "images," and then he felt ill.

She looked so scared. The camera flashes made her look pale, and her eyes were huge. One picture showed her looking back over her shoulder as she ran. Another caught her head-on with her blonde hair flying out behind her straw hat. What had become of that hat? Was it still in the back of his truck? Or had it blown off somewhere along 14A? And for that matter, what had happened to that *dress*? The dress he was looking at in the pictures was *not* the pretty dress she had been wearing when he pulled her out of his truck. Not even close.

This thing in the picture looked like a shiny black tube that they'd somehow sewn her into. It couldn't have been comfortable. And yet she was running in it. Running like a woman in danger.

What could Mindy Rose possibly have to be afraid of? This question made his mind swim with entertaining possibilities. Maybe she was a criminal, and she was running from the cops. Probably not. If that were the case, she never would have gone on stage, right? Or maybe she'd seen some other criminal in the crowd, and she'd been running from *him*. Or her.

Or maybe she had some psycho fan after her, a dangerous stalker. He dismissed this idea as soon as he had it. If that was the case, she would have told the police. Maybe she was insane, and she'd been running from some monster that didn't exist. This theory didn't ring true, though. No, he didn't know her, and yet, he couldn't make himself believe that she was crazy.

Debts! That could be it! He knew that rich people could be just as stupid with money as poor people. Maybe she was in gambling trouble and some loan shark had come to break her fingers. Or maybe she had a drug problem. He forced himself to look up from his phone. He felt guilty for thinking such seedy things about her. She'd seemed so nice, so real, so innocent when she'd been wearing a purple dress and calling herself Mandy.

He turned his screen off and tried to focus on the message, but without even realizing that he was doing it, he went back to scrolling.

He landed on a picture of her while she was still on stage. *Whoa.* She did not look so good. She was bent over like she was going to be sick.

Her microphone lay by her feet. He felt so bad for her then. Whatever was going on, it really wasn't fun for her.

Seth elbowed him. Dustin expected he did so because he was about to scold him, but Seth showed him his phone instead. He'd found a video. Dustin pressed play. There she was in all her well-lit glory. She was singing with one arm in the air, looking like any other country star on any other stage, but then her lips stopped moving. Seth had the phone on silent, but Dustin still felt like he could hear it, the sudden loss of lyrics. She stared at the fans in front of her. She looked confused. Then she staggered a few steps to her right, got control of her feet, and then looked up at the lights beating down on her. She turned and looked at her drummer. Dustin couldn't see his face in the video, but he was confident that's who she was looking at.

She staggered again and then bent over and put her hands on her knees. Her guitar player tried to come to her aid, but she shrugged him off. Then she was looking around again. Here the camera got wobbly as if someone bumped into the filmmaker, but it steadied itself in time to see Mindy take off running toward the back of the stage.

And then she just vanished. Like a magic trick.

Dustin looked up from the phone and into Seth's face. "Wow," he mouthed, and Seth nodded his agreement. Only then did Dustin realize that Wyatt must have let Seth in on the little secret. He turned to give Wyatt a dirty look, but his eyes met Ma Bannon's, who was staring at him reproachfully. She didn't like it when people were on their phones in church. His cheeks got hot, and he focused on the pastor for the rest of the sermon.

Chapter 9

Mindy wasn't sure what to do with herself as she waited for the Honeywood brothers to come inside. At least, she assumed it was more than just Hudson out there, unless he was talking to himself. She felt incredibly conspicuous standing all alone in their living room, like she'd been caught doing something bad. Well, maybe she had. Maybe shirking all one's responsibilities was a bad thing.

Her mother had raised her better than this. She tried to swallow the lump that was forming in her throat. She needed to figure this out.

"Hey!" Dustin said when he saw her. He looked genuinely excited to see her.

"Good morning, Mandy," Hudson said. For a second, she thought he'd forgotten her name. Then she remembered that she'd stupidly picked an alias only one letter off from her real name. It was a good thing she wasn't a criminal—she would be really bad at it.

"Good morning." She tried to sound like a normal person instead of a famous fugitive. She smiled at Dustin. "Or rather, afternoon. Sorry that I slept so late. I didn't mean to. It's been a really long time since I've had a good night's sleep. I swear I'm not a lazy grifter." She made herself stop talking.

Dustin was staring at her. "It never occurred to me that you were lazy or a grifter."

"If you're a grifter," Hudson said, "you picked the wrong ranch." He chuckled. "It would be one low-paying con job."

She concentrated on her breathing. It was weird enough that she was just standing there in the middle of their house. If she collapsed from lack of oxygen, they might decide she was too bizarre to help any further. She opened her mouth to ask to use Dustin's phone, forgot what she was going to say, and said, "How was church?" instead. She hadn't been to a real church service in years. She very much missed going with her mother and then going out to lunch afterward.

"It was church," Dustin said, totally taking it for granted.

"That's nice." *Oh my gosh, why are you so lame, Mindy?* Her embarrassment brought her to her senses. "Dustin, could I please borrow your phone? I think my friend is probably awake by now." She laughed stupidly.

He took his phone out of his pocket. "You're welcome to use this, or there's a land line right there on the desk if you'd rather."

"Uh, I think I'd like to take it outside if you don't mind."

"Oh, of course," he said quickly. "You'll want some privacy. My bad." He closed the gap between them and held the phone out to her. She felt his presence getting closer like an energy field. This guy was a magnet, and she was a little lost piece of iron floating around in the sea. Resisting his pull, she took the phone from his hand, thanked him, and stepped outside.

She nearly gasped at the beauty of it. For starters, it was a *gorgeous* day. And secondly, this property was majestic. Rolling fields stretched in all directions with a big old butte in the distance standing over the grasses like a stalwart sentinel. A burbling creek weaved its way through the property, and somewhere nearby birds were chirping. The smell of grass rode the breeze, and she just froze there for a moment, breathing in the wonder of the place. No wonder they'd tried to make it into an event center. Once they had their rooms ready, surely they would get bookings.

She dialed the familiar phone number from Keely's youth, and no one answered. She wondered if they were screening their calls and tried again. Her dad answered in a huff, likely expecting a foreign accent threatening an IRS audit. "Hi, Mr. McCurdy." She quickly strode toward the pasture. "This is Mindy Rose. I was wondering—"

"Mindy! Are you okay, sweetheart?"

So, they'd heard. Ugh. Maybe she should have done an internet search on herself before she started making her calls. "Yes, I'm okay. And please don't tell anyone that I called—"

"What's wrong, sweetheart?"

"Who is it, Chad?" Keely's mom asked in the background.

"It's Mindy!" he shouted.

Mindy winced.

"She's okay!" he hollered.

"Oh! ... relief to hear! You tell her ... praying for her!" Mindy could hear her getting closer to the phone. "Ask her what on earth happened!"

"Mr. McCurdy?" she hurriedly broke in. "I'll tell you all about it just as soon as I can, but right now I really need to talk to Keely—"

"Yes, of course. Where is she?"

What? "Uh, I don't know, but—"

"She should be pretty near through Mississippi by now."

What? "Can you remind me of her phone number, please? I've lost my phone."

"You lost your phone? Oh dear! Keely would lose her mind if she ever lost her phone. Did someone steal yours, you think?"

She ground her teeth together. She loved these people, but right now ... "I really need to talk to her. Could I have the number please?" Too late she realized she had nothing to write with or on. She ripped open Dustin's truck door and started poking through the nooks and crannies. She didn't find anything, and knowing it was an incredibly rude and invasive thing to do, she opened the glove box. There. Three pens. She grabbed one and wrote the number on her arm as Mr. McCurdy recited it.

She thanked him and tried to hang up, but he wasn't having it. "Do you need anything else, sweetheart?"

"No, thank you. I will—"

"You know you are always welcome to stay here with us if you need a place to go."

"I know. Thank you." *I'm twenty-five and rich, but thanks.*

She finally managed to get off the phone and immediately dialed Keely's number. Then she waited impatiently as it rang. With a start, she saw Chase staring at her from a distance, and she jumped to return the pen, shut the glove box, and slam the truck door shut. But it didn't matter. She'd been caught being rude and invasive. She hoped he would blame it on the chaos swirling around inside her.

Keely answered, and the phone speaker filled with the sound of wind. Speaker phone.

"I'm okay."

"Mindy!" she cried. "Where are you?"

"I'm still in South Dakota. Where are you?"

"I'm on my way, sista. Just crossed the mighty Mississip."

Mindy laughed. It was so good to hear her friend's voice. "I appreciate that, and I will pay you back for every penny. How did you know I was going to need you to come?"

She laughed too. "I didn't, but what was I supposed to do, sit home on my bum while you were in crisis? I was going crazy, so I just started driving." The mirth fell out of her voice. "Mindy, I was really scared. What happened?"

"Honestly?" She sighed. "Nothing really. I can't explain it. I just totally freaked out."

There was a hesitation. "Like was there some guy or ..."

"No, no. It was like a panic attack, but ... well, it was pretty bad." Calling it a panic attack made it seem so much less scary than it had been. "I don't know what it was, but I had to get out of there. I couldn't breathe."

"Okay," she said slowly.

Mindy didn't want to explain. She would sound like such a brat if she complained about the downside of having all her dreams come true. Even she didn't want to listen to that. "Anyway, I don't know what I'm going to do, but I am totally stranded right now at some random ranch in South Dakota, and I don't have my wallet or my phone. So I could use a lift."

"A lift where?"

"I don't know yet, but for starters, a lift off this ranch."

Another hesitation. "I'm coming for you, sista, but if I drive straight through, I won't be there till tomorrow, and I don't think I can drive straight through and make it there alive. I mean, I'll try, but I'm not sure there's enough coffee in the world—"

"No, no, be safe." She looked at the house, and at the spot that the outdoor brother had now vacated. "I think I'm okay here till tomorrow. If not, I can call you back with a plan B."

She laughed. "Is there anyone else you could call? I mean, I know I'm your favorite, but I also know you have other friends. Like thousands of them. Surely one of them is closer? Not that I don't want to be the hero. I do, but I'm trying to think of you here."

"And that's why I need *you*, Keely, because you'll think of me. I don't have thousands of friends. I have thousands of acquaintances who would tattle on me the first chance they got." She sighed. "I will let you know if I think of a better plan, but for right now, please set your GPS to West Hope, South Dakota."

"Aww, what a lovely name for a town."

"Yes, it is. I haven't actually seen the town yet, but what I'm looking at here on the outskirts is sure lovely."

"Which half of the state is it on?"

"Sorry. The west half."

She groaned.

"I know, I know. I'll make it up to you, I promise."

"I want to meet Luke Bryan."

"I'll see what I can do." She didn't even know Luke Bryan.

"I mean *meet* him. Like shake his hand and have a conversation."

"Sure. I should go. This isn't my phone—"

"Is it the rancher's? Is he single?"

"I ... uh ... think he is. But ..."

"But what?"

"Look, we've got a long ride back, and I'll fill you in then."

"Long ride back to Alabama? I thought you said you didn't know where you were going?"

She understood why her friend had so many questions, but she didn't have any answers yet. "Keely, I love you, but I need some time to figure this out, okay? Thank you for coming to get me. I promise I will make it up to you."

"Okay. Luke Bryan."

"Yeah, yeah." She said goodbye and hung up. She wasn't going to be able to orchestrate any big celebrity meet if she transformed herself from Nashville's doll into Nashville's pariah. She started back toward the house but then had another idea.

She typed her name into the search bar and then gasped. *Oh no.* She'd known there would be pictures, but these were really *bad* pictures. Her publicist was going to completely spazz out. And the head-

Chapter 10

Dustin watched Mindy come inside. She didn't look happy. "Is everything okay?"

She hesitated before answering. "Yeah. Everything is fine. Thank you for asking. But I'm really sorry to say that my friend can't get here until tomorrow." She looked at the floor. "I hate being a mooch, but could I stay here one more night? I will definitely pay you once I get my... once I can get myself organized."

Dustin looked at Hudson, waiting for him to answer, but Hudson was looking at him.

"Of course, you're welcome to stay here," Dustin said. "And no payment necessary." She was going to need some supplies. If she were an ordinary woman stranded at the ranch, he would invite her to go to Walmart for a little shopping spree. But she wasn't about to walk into Walmart. Of course, he could deepen his ruse by inviting her anyway, knowing that she'd say no. But that felt deceptive, so he didn't invite her. This was too bad, as he would have enjoyed the excuse to spend time with her. "I was just about to make a Walmart run."

Hudson didn't try to hide his surprise. They had just been in town when they'd gone to church. Dustin's cheeks got warm again. He had blushed more in the last twenty-four hours than he had since high school. Obviously, he didn't spend enough time around beautiful women. There weren't very many of them working at the water district, and all the ones at church were already taken. He shook his head to clear his thoughts. "I'm not much of an expert on women's fashion, but would you like me to pick you up a few things?"

It was obvious that she did want that. But she thanked him and said no.

"I really don't mind." He didn't want to beg, but he knew that she wanted him to do it.

"I feel like a helpless child without my purse. I can't let you go buy me clothes."

"It's okay," Hudson said. "Dustin here is an engineer. He's rolling in the cash." He laughed at his own joke.

Dustin's embarrassment deepened. While he did make a comfortable living, he was standing toe to toe with someone who probably had a million dollars in the bank. "I'm a *civil* engineer who works in *public water* in *South Dakota.* Anyway ..." He turned his attention back to Mindy.

"You make it sound like that's not impressive. As far as I know, it is. I flunked geometry, so I think all engineers are impressive. And water's pretty important, especially in South Dakota."

Dustin didn't know what to say to that.

"Well, look at that, Dustin." Hudson laughed obnoxiously. "You've got a fan!"

Oh, the irony. He cleared his throat. "Anyway, if you're comfortable in that dress, I'm comfortable too. But if you'd like some variety and maybe some pajamas and maybe a toothbrush—"

Her hand flew to her mouth self-consciously, and he wished he hadn't said that last part. He hurried to keep talking and bury the awkwardness in his words' wake. "I would be happy to go fill a bag for you. If it makes you feel any better, you can send me a check once you get situated, but that's not necessary either."

Her eyes lit up. "That's a great idea!" She nodded. "I will send you a check." This was adorable. She was actually excited. She looked at Hudson. "For all of it. For everything."

"Do you want me to write me a list?"

"Do you have the Walmart app on your phone?"

No, of course he didn't. He wasn't a soccer mom. Why would he have the Walmart app on his phone?

"I've got it on mine," Hudson said. "Why, what do you need?"

She giggled. "I was going to give him a list like adding things to his cart, but you don't have to give him your phone. I can just use a pencil and do it the old-fashioned way." She looked around the kitchen. "Do you have a pencil I could borrow?"

Dustin woke up his phone. "You know, I've been really meaning to download the Walmart app. Let me do that for you." He sat down at the table, and she sat nearby. He watched the spinning circle. "Sorry, don't have the best cell service around here."

"But it sure is gorgeous." Her sincerity was noticeable. Poor thing, she'd been around too many neon lights.

"It certainly is," Hudson said. "That's why I wanted to live here. And I haven't taken a single day for granted since we moved in."

Her eyebrows lifted. "You didn't grow up around here?"

"We did," Hudson said, "but we grew up in town, in West Hope. But Chase and I wanted to have some land for horses. Not that people don't squeeze horses onto town lots." He chuckled. "But more room means happier horses."

"And more horses," Dustin added, thinking of Chase.

"That's awesome that you get to live with your sibling. I wish I could live with my sister, but I—" She abruptly stopped talking. She had almost shared too much.

Dustin felt desperate to help her save face. "Sibling relationships are hard. We were fortunate in that our mother put up with literally zero fighting. We learned to work things out peacefully, or she would make us regret it pretty quickly."

She smiled politely, but her eyes were full of regret.

"Oh look!" Dustin tried to sound excited. "It's downloaded." He handed her the phone and then tried not to stare at her as she shopped virtually. After a few minutes she sighed and shook her head. "Individually these things seem so cheap, but it's really adding up."

He put his hand over hers, and she looked up in surprise. "Will you please just let me do this? It will bless me to help you."

"He's for real," Hudson interjected, and Dustin wished he'd go away, but it was his kitchen. "Dustin's a pretty helpful guy."

"Seems like all the Honeywoods are pretty helpful," she said softly. She looked out the window. "It makes sense why you would want to invite people here and help them out that way."

Hudson chuckled. "Oh, that was just for the money."

She looked bewildered.

Dustin laughed. "He's kind of joking, but Chase does have quite a horse habit—"

"Don't put it like that," Hudson said. "She'll think he's addicted to heroin."

Now Dustin really wanted him to go away no matter whose kitchen it was. "Horse means heroin?"

It was clear that Mindy knew that. "That interpretation never would have occurred to me," she said. "I saw the horses. I knew what you meant. So you're opening an event center to fund his horse habit?" She seemed charmed by this, and a pang of jealousy hit Dustin's chest. This was silly and embarrassing. If Mindy Rose fell madly in love with Chase, then good for Chase. But Dustin still didn't want that to happen. Chase barely even liked music. Of course, that might be exactly what Mindy needed. Who was he to say?

"Yes, Chase wants to breed horses, so Olivia had this brilliant idea to host weddings here."

"I really like Olivia." Now she sounded regretful again.

"We all do," Dustin said.

Mindy slid the phone across the table. "There's your cart. Thank you so much."

He picked the phone up and stood. "No worries. Be back in a jiffy."

Chapter 11

Mindy felt a little weird sitting around the house with Hudson. She really, really wished she'd had the presence of mind to grab her phone before running away from her life. Then at least she'd have something to fiddle with. She could play Hay Day all day. But she didn't have her phone, so she was staring at the wall. Poor Hudson was trying to have a nice, lazy Sunday afternoon, and here she was interloping. They were being so nice to her, not acting annoyed at all, but still—she felt annoying. She was almost annoyed for them. She was annoying herself. She almost snorted at the thought.

Hudson looked up, and she got up quickly.

"Would you mind if I went and wandered around your property?" She laughed uncomfortably.

"Not at all. Make yourself at home. But just so you know, Chase is out there." He laughed. "I didn't mean to make that sound ominous. He just doesn't make much noise. I didn't want you to round a corner and get a Hollywood-worthy jump scare."

She laughed. "Thanks for the warning. Do you have any estimation of when Dustin might be back? I want to be here when he gets here." She winced. That had sounded far less needy in her head.

"I don't know, but it might be a while. West Hope doesn't have a Walmart, so I'm guessing he went all the way to Spearfish."

"Oh. Okay. Thanks." What a bummer. She could have ridden with him—*no, you couldn't have because he would have asked you why you were ducking down in the parking lot.*

The sunlight greeted her like an old friend who was really excited to see her. She closed her eyes and turned her face up to greet it. It warmed her whole body; she could almost feel it healing her, refueling her. She opened her eyes so she could walk without accidentally smashing into Chase, but she still paid attention to that feeling of the sun on her skin. She didn't get nearly enough time outdoors anymore. For a kid who grew up bass fishing and plucking cornflowers, she sure had turned into a city girl. She looked down at her dress and realized that it was the color of Alabama cornflowers—no wonder she liked it so much.

These days she was often on her bus all day or holed up in some hotel. She loved the outdoor festivals, but even then she didn't get to do much sunbathing. She always had to be squirreled away somewhere so that people couldn't get to her without paying a surcharge.

She hated it.

She hated her life.

How had it come to this?

Instantly, she felt guilty. *Stop feeling sorry for yourself.* There were thousands upon thousands of dedicated, talented musicians who would kill for a shot at her life. She had been one of them not very long ago. But this ... this wasn't what she thought it would be like. She'd gotten into this because she loved music. Now, she missed the music.

The melody of the creek beckoned her, and she headed that way. Trees grew sporadically along each bank, and their bright green leaves were so gorgeous they nearly took her breath away. This was quite a different scene from her creeks back home, which were so overgrown they seemed to disappear into the forest. It could be impossible to follow one without walking down the middle of it. How had she seen the entire country, a third of Canada, and some of Europe—and not seen a single creek till now?

Or maybe she had, and she just didn't remember. If she did get back on the road, she vowed to pay more attention to the creeks.

She started back toward the house. Dustin would be back soon. If a Walmart run would take much longer, then he never would have gone on it. She went around the back side of the house, taking the scenic route, and as she came around the corner, she thought she heard him, and her heart leapt with excitement. She had only seconds to analyze why she was quite so excited when she caught sight of the vehicle, and it definitely was not his.

It was a tomato-colored Cadillac SUV. It was the size of a house. Shiny, iridescent ketchup.

Just looking at it made her want some fries with that.

And just when it couldn't get any stranger, the world's oldest pickup truck pulled in behind it. But it wasn't one pickup truck so much as several pickup trucks cobbled together. There was a two-foot gap between the tires and the body, which made it tower over the Cadillac. Maybe that was the driver's intention.

A woman in a skirt suit slid gracefully out of the Cadillac. A normal-looking young man in khakis got out of the other side. Then an incredibly tall man with a ponytail, dressed head to toe in camo, got out of the truck. He was with a beautiful young woman who sported many colorful tattoos—from Mindy's vantage point, they looked like butterflies. As Mindy was admiring her from afar, the back of the truck's cap opened up, and two young teen boys sprang out. They looked positively feral. The woman in the skirt suit gasped and clutched the chunky beads around her neck.

Mindy had to stop staring. As entertaining as this was—whatever this was—she couldn't afford to get caught out in the open. Assuming that they were headed toward the house, she crouched down and ran toward the barn. If they looked in her direction, they would see her, but they all seemed pretty self-absorbed.

She ducked into the cool dim light of the barn and leaned back against the wall to wait, genuinely disappointed that she was going to miss the rest of the show. She could still hear their voices, and she strained to make out what they were saying:

A woman: Not much parking.

A man: Park on the road.

Someone said something she couldn't make out. She thought it was Hudson.

Whatever he'd said, a woman said, "Well how many can you accommodate?"

Misty didn't hear the answer to this, but she finally figured out what was happening. This improbably diverse group of people was looking for an event center. Mindy put a hand over her mouth for backup in case she couldn't hold in the giggle. She had no reason to think that these people were looking for a *wedding* venue, but she really, really hoped they were. She desperately wanted the beautiful young woman with the tattoos to be marrying the nice-looking young man from the Cadillac. She was a sucker for an opposites attract romance. Although Dustin didn't seem to be all that different from her, and she was plenty attracted to him.

"How many restrooms do you have?"

This time she could hear Hudson. "There will be three, and we can bring in portable toilets if we need—"

"Porta potties?" a woman shrieked. "I can't ask our guests to use an *outhouse*!"

"Mom, stop," someone said. Probably the guy in khakis.

Mindy was so focused on her eavesdropping that she didn't realize the voices were growing closer until it was almost too late. She looked around in a panic, but there was nowhere to hide. A ladder to her left led up to a loft, and she scaled it like a gecko on amphetamines. She still had two rungs to go when they walked into the barn, but no one looked up. She pulled her feet up and into the shadows and then held very, very still.

The loft was very small, much smaller than a normal loft. Farmers of years gone by would have been able to store a dozen bales in this small space, maybe. And though it was difficult to see up here, the wall to her left looked new. She surmised that they had shrunk the loft during renovations, which made sense if they were putting lodging in this thing.

"Caleb, it's just a *barn*!"

Misty couldn't stand not watching. She would rather risk being seen than miss this. She pulled herself into a squat, and her toe accidentally knocked a chunk of hay and dust over the edge. She gasped before she could get that hand back up to her mouth again.

"What was that?" Ms. Ketchup Cadillac said, her voice full of fear. At least Mindy thought it was her. She didn't think Pretty Tattoo Girl would frighten that easily.

A loud bang sounded on the other side of the barn, and a man's gruff voice said, "Stevie, get down from there."

"No!" Stevie shouted.

Slowly, Mindy peeked out over the edge. And there they were. Mr. Khakis stood between Pretty Tattoo Girl and Mrs. Ketchup Cadillac, and Mindy had never felt so sorry for anyone in her life. Mr. Ponytail stood off to the edge, slightly ostracized. His eyes were on the boy trying to climb the chain on the wall. That must be Stevie.

The other boy carried what looked like a ping-pong paddle. For the first time, Mindy was a little scared. She wasn't sure Hudson was safe down there. Where on earth was Chase? She would feel a lot better if Chase were there.

"I think I've seen enough," Mrs. Ketchup Cadillac said.

"Mom, it's not really up to you," Mr. Khakis said.

His mother spun on him. Mindy couldn't see her face now, but she could feel the heat of her glare coming out the back of her head. "If I'm the one paying for it, then I would say it is very much up to me!"

Mr. Khaki's face registered pain, and Pretty Tattoo Girl slid her hand into his and softly said. "It's okay. We can go."

"No." To his credit, Mr. Khakis had some intestinal fortitude going for him. "You want a ranch wedding, and we're going to give you a ranch wedding."

Pretty Tattoo Girl laid her cheek against her fiancé's shoulder and avoided her mother-in-law-to-be's eyes.

Mindy was hit by three strong emotions at once: jealousy; the joy of being completely entertained; and an insane desire to pop up and declare that she would be paying for their wedding. It was so tempting that she almost did it.

Something warm caressed her arm, and she let out a short shriek. She turned to see that somehow, Dustin had joined her. How she hadn't heard him coming, she couldn't imagine. How he'd gotten up there, she couldn't imagine. He certainly hadn't come up the ladder.

"What was *that*?" Ms. Ketchup Cadillac asked.

"Probably just a mouse." Hudson glared in her direction, and their eyes met briefly before she yanked her head back into the shadows. So Hudson knew she was up here. And he was annoyed. This made the whole thing less fun, and she was suddenly motivated to start behaving herself. She stayed back in the shadows, resisting the urge to peek out over the edge anymore.

It was hard to make out Dustin's face with so little light, but she could feel the confusion coming off him in waves.

Hudson wisely led his prospective clients deeper into the barn as Ms. Ketchup Cadillac continued to complain.

Dustin woke up his phone screen and started typing. She hoped he was texting Chase to get in here for backup. Why Dustin hadn't offered backup instead of climbing up into the loft via some secret ladder, she didn't know. He held the phone up for her to see. "Why are you up here?" Oh, he was texting *her*.

For a second she didn't understand the question. She was hiding, of course. But then she remembered that Dustin didn't know who she was. He only knew she liked to hide in uncomfortable places. She took his phone, intent on giving his completely reasonable question an answer, but then she couldn't come up with one.

The voices drifted deeper and deeper into the barn, and Mindy's legs started to cramp. She tried to adjust them, which put her even closer to Dustin, if that were possible. Now her hip was pressed against his. She gave up and handed the phone back to him without typing anything. It was okay if he thought she was a nut. She would be leaving in the morning.

Chapter 12

D ustin could not come up with any reasonable explanation for why Mindy was hiding in the loft. Had Hudson lost his mind, spilled the beans, and told her to hide? No, because if he had, he would have given her a much better spot.

Dustin wished he'd thought it through before coming up here. He hadn't realized the quarters would be quite so ... *tight*. She was like a gorgeous ball of warm energy beside him. It didn't help that the small space was growing hotter by the second between the June heat rising and their own body heat doing its thing. He wanted to take his hat off and mop his brow, but there wasn't enough room.

And what was she *doing*? Why was she spying on these weirdos Hudson was trying to recruit? Dustin had only seen them for ten seconds and knew he should start praying that they would choose *not* to have their wedding here. Chase was going to have a complete meltdown.

He had to get out of here. This loft was stupid anyway. It was a fake loft. A decorative loft. Wyatt had converted most of the real loft into lodging, but Hudson had insisted they keep some of it open so people could look up and see hay.

Why was she so close to him? And was she getting closer? Yes, yes, she was, and then her lips were pressed to his, and he was so surprised that he started to tip backward. His arm flailed, accidentally caught hers, and because she was still pushing with her lips, they both toppled backward into a small pile of hay. This would have been a soft, poetic landing, but the space was too small, and he rapped the back of his head on the wall, knocking his hat forward so it balanced atop both their heads. They were sharing his hat. The contact hurt enough to make a man yelp, but his *ow* was muffled by her kiss.

Somewhere, far beneath them, in a whole different world, an unpleasant female voice asked, "What was *that*?"

Despite his pain he was kissing Mindy back rather enthusiastically. How could he not? She was gorgeous, talented, and charming. *But she thinks you're kissing Mandy.* This thought pricked his conscience, and he gently pushed her off him.

Beneath them: "I've seen enough! Caleb, let's go!"

"Mom, wait!"

The multiple footsteps suggested that Mom was not waiting.

Neither was Mindy. She had untangled herself from him and was pushed as far from him—and as close to the edge of the artificial loft—as possible. Knowing full well it would annoy her, he couldn't help reaching out and gently tugging her a little closer to him. If Mindy Rose broke her neck falling off Hudson's stupid ornamental loft, it would be more than Dustin could bear. She moved less than an inch, but it was something.

When the barn fell silent, he whispered, "Why are you up here?"

She turned her shoulders away from him and reached for the ladder, but she was at a terrible angle to start down the ladder. And he was very much in the way of her turning herself around.

He gently touched her arm. "I can show you another way down."

She nodded, still averting her eyes. He'd hurt her feelings, which was a terrible development. He hadn't wanted to stop kissing her. He'd done that only to protect her feelings, but everything was so twisted because she was pretending to be someone she wasn't. Or at least pretending not to be who she was.

He pushed the mostly invisible door open and slid out into a hallway. He then turned to offer a hand, which she ignored. She slowly straightened, obviously having stiffened up from her little one-woman game of hide and seek. She turned and looked down at the door, which only reached their waist. "Why does this barn have a little Coraline door?"

He didn't know what a Coraline door was but figured it was some kind of fancy southern thing. "Hudson asked for it. He didn't want to be carrying hay bales up that ladder."

"Oh. Okay, so how do we get out of here?"

So she wasn't going to tell him why she was up there? Cool. He turned and showed her the way out. A narrow hallway ran down the center of the loft to another set of stairs in the back of the barn. They descended these stairs in silence and then walked the length of the barn again to get back to the front door.

Just before he stepped outside, she said, "Are they gone?" He knew full well why she was asking, but she explained, "I'm just really shy."

Stop lying, he wanted to say, but he also had no idea what her life was like and tried to be patient. "Okay." He stuck his head through the door. "No, not yet. But it looks like she's trying to herd them up."

"She is an awful human being."

"You got that impression too, huh? And I have never seen a vehicle that red. It almost defies the physics of color."

She snorted and then quickly covered her mouth.

"Hey," he said softly, "I'm sorry about before. It's not that I didn't want to kiss you—"

"Not an issue," she said firmly. "My friend will be here in the morning." She stared out through the open door, her jaw set.

"Hey, don't be like that. I just … I would like to get to know you better—"

"Like I said, not an issue." She turned away. "I'm going to go wait over there." She headed to the end of the barn they'd just come from.

He could have left, but he didn't. He waited till the hideous wedding party was gone and then he hollered out, "The coast is clear" before stepping out into the daylight. He grabbed the plastic shopping bags out of the back of his truck on the way by. He'd been so proud of his haul. He'd really tried to get it right, getting her everything he could think of that she might need or want. He'd even gotten her some fancy chocolates to ease her stress.

She came into the house five minutes after him, and he looked at the kitchen table. "I put your things there."

Her face lit up, but it was a weird light, an artificial light. She was performing for him. She smiled brightly. "Thank you so much. You're too kind."

He almost flinched. Seriously? After all this, she was going to give him her *stage* smile? Gross. Maybe Mindy Rose wasn't the sweet country girl he'd thought she was. Maybe all of her was an act. One big, gross act. Dustin gave the biggest, most clownish smile he could, showing more teeth than a horse, and said, "Golly, you're so welcome. It was my pleasure!"

Her eyes grew wide as the smile slowly fell off her face and bewilderment took its place.

He grabbed a drink out of the fridge and headed for the television.

Chapter 13

M indy watched Dustin go into the living room. No man had ever sassed her like that. Ever.

It made her like him even more.

She hadn't meant to kiss him, but he'd been so close, and he didn't know who she was, and she'd thought right then that she might never again get to kiss a man who wasn't kissing her back for her money or her fame. Despite pretty good looks, she'd never been much of a heartthrob, certainly not once she landed in Nashville, where she never managed to turn a single head.

But then once the success rolled in, they started showing up. And it was all so fake.

But this guy—this water engineer from the middle of nowhere South Dakota who listened to ancient music and couldn't carry a tune in a bucket—he actually seemed to like *her*. Her without the fame. Her without the money. Her without the sequins. So she'd thought it might be her only chance to kiss someone who really wanted to kiss *her.* And for a second, she'd been right. At first, it was the kiss of the ages, making fireworks explode in her brain, but then he'd pushed her away.

And she didn't know why.

And now she was stuck here. Stuck here with Mr. Sassy Water Guy.

And it was a long time till morning. They hadn't even had supper yet.

"What did you think, Mandy?" Hudson loudly asked from the living room. He was being friendly, inviting her to hang out with them, trying to include her, and she couldn't run away. Where was she going to go?

She gingerly entered the living room. "What do I think about what?"

"Settle a bet. Dustin here says those people aren't going to be worth the money. I say that all money spends the same. What do you think?"

Her throat was as dry as an expired dog biscuit, but she swallowed anyway. "I'm not sure. Did they say they were going to have their wedding here?"

Hudson chuckled heartily. "No, they sure didn't. They were still arguing when they left, so I suppose there's still hope, but no, they didn't leave a deposit check." He tipped his head back and closed his eyes. "Just like all the others. This seemed like such a good idea until I tried actually getting bookings." He picked his head up and looked at her. "And then they all say no. We're actually going *further* into the hole instead of digging out of it."

She stood there awkwardly.

He motioned to the couch, which Dustin already occupied one end of. "Come on, join us. What do you do for work?"

Shoot, she hadn't invented this part of the lie yet. She sat slowly to give herself time to think of something.

"You look like a woman in sales."

"I do?"

"Sure. But I meant it as a compliment. I would buy something from you. But no? Not in sales?"

He was right. She *was* in sales. She'd never wanted to be, but somehow, that's where she had ended up. "I'm a waitress," she spit out. She wasn't sure, but it looked like Dustin choked back a laugh. She glared at him. Did he have something against waitresses?

Hudson nodded. "I can see that, and I wasn't so far off. Plenty of waitresses have convinced me to order more food." He chuckled and rubbed his stomach, though there was no extra weight there at all. All of these men looked like they worked out. Maybe they had a gym in their basement.

"Your accent makes it clear you're from the south, but where exactly?"

Oh boy. She knew he was just being friendly, making conversation, but this was a slippery slope. "Alabama."

He didn't seem surprised. "And you came all the way from Alabama just for Wild Bill Days?"

"Yeah."

"Must have been a big fan of one of the bands playing? Who'd they have this year?"

Her stomach rolled.

"So where did you find those terrible potential customers?" Dustin quickly asked.

She looked at Dustin with curiosity. Had that been a deliberate redirect? And if so, why had he done it? Had he sensed that she hadn't wanted to talk? Or was something else going on?

Hudson laughed. "I didn't find them. They found me. The bride-to-be called and asked if she and her father could come see the place. I didn't expect the groom and his lovely mother."

"Yikes," Dustin said.

"Yeah. And have you ever seen a vehicle that color? Good grief."

"No," Dustin said. "I sure haven't."

Hudson looked at Mindy again. "You really didn't need to hide from them. It would have been okay for them to see you in there. I didn't promise them an exclusive tour or anything."

Mindy opened her mouth to lie again, but Dustin didn't give her the chance. "She's really shy," he said as he tried to stare a hole through the floor.

Chapter 14

Dustin knocked tentatively on the guest room door. Mindy hadn't said a word during supper, and then she'd immediately gone into her room. If she was snoozing, he didn't want to wake her. But he also didn't want her to go to bed with hurt feelings. While he knew he had no chance at an actual future with Mindy Rose, he never wanted to hurt any woman's feelings.

He heard rustling, and then the door cracked open.

"Hi." He felt like a timid schoolboy with a crush.

"Hi," she said softly.

"No pressure, don't feel obligated, but I was going to watch a movie, and I wondered if you wanted to join me. I could make popcorn?"

She took her time considering it, and just when he was sure she was going to decline, she said, "Sure." She stepped out and shut the door behind her.

"I don't have much to offer for toppings. Hudson is kind of a health nut, so he puts weird things on popcorn."

She furrowed her brow. "Toppings? On popcorn?"

"Well, yeah. They have those flavored powders you sprinkle on. And some people use chocolate. He might have chocolate."

"In Alabama, we use butter."

He smiled. "If he has real butter, we'll have Chase to thank for that. I'll check." He headed for the fridge. He was pretty sure that stores in Alabama sold popcorn toppings, but it was cute that she thought there was really only one option.

Hudson and Chase *did* have some butter. It was the good stuff too. Local and Irish. He got the popcorn maker out and tried not to be nervous. *This isn't a date, you idiot. You're just watching a movie.*

But she'd sat on the couch, not in the recliner.

Don't read anything into that. It has a better angle at the television.

He carried the giant bowl into the living room agonizing over where to sit—but when he reached her, he realized he had to sit right beside her, or she wasn't going to get any popcorn.

So he sat, silently begging his heart to stop beating so fast. He was afraid she'd hear it and call an ambulance.

"Okay, what do you want to watch?"

She looked surprised. "You haven't picked yet?"

"No, but we've got a lot of choices." He started scrolling through.

"Let's watch something scary."

This surprised him. "Really?"

"Yeah. Like super terrifying."

He wasn't sure he wanted to do that. He'd already screamed like an about-to-be-murdered teenage girl when he'd found her in his truck. He didn't want to get caught being a screamer again.

But she looked amused, and this challenged him. "Uh ... okay." He typed *scary* into the search bar and then flinched when he saw the options. *Good grief, the movie hasn't even started yet.*

"Not like slasher gory bloody scary. Those aren't actually scary."

He thought they were, but he didn't argue.

"Like ... *psychologically* terrifying."

He handed her the remote. "Here. You pick."

"Are you sure?"

"Yep."

"Are you sure you trust me?"

He looked at her. What, was she flirting with him? "I don't know. But you can pick."

She laughed like he'd said something hysterical and then turned her attention to the scrolling. She went on forever, and he was starting to think he was going to fall asleep before the movie started, so he started eating the popcorn.

"No! You have to wait for the movie."

"Then hurry up and pick. Your precious butter is solidifying."

She laughed again. "Good grief, you are a sassy man."

The word sassy didn't exactly sound masculine, but he accepted it. It had probably been a while since any man had talked back to her. It was likely that she rarely saw anyone who didn't work for her or wasn't a raving fan.

"There." She pressed play, and he braced himself.

When he realized the movie was about a super-fan tormenting a celebrity, Dustin tried to study Mindy without getting caught. Why on earth had she picked *this*? Was it a coincidence, or did she have some crazy super-fan after her? Was that who she was running from? This didn't make sense because she had a herd of people with her, people who could protect her. Wait! What if the super-fan was *one of her own people*? This theory excited him for several seconds until he realized that she must have enough money to hire real security to protect her from anyone—even someone on the inside. Then he remembered how some country singers have had to sue in order to get the money that was owed them. Maybe Mindy wasn't rich. Maybe she was just making money for someone else. That might be a good reason to run away too. She might have gotten tired of that arrangement. But still, wouldn't it be easier to get a lawyer? He hated the fact that she was going to leave tomorrow, and he was never going to get any answers. Unsolved mysteries annoyed him. Maybe he could reveal the truth right before she got into her friend's car. He could say, "Hey I know who you are, and I promise not to tell anyone you were here, but *please* tell me why you were here so it doesn't drive me insane!"

That wasn't a half-bad idea, and he'd pretty much settled on it when she caught him staring and said, "What?"

"Oh nothing," he said quickly and glanced at the screen, where the super-fan was shaving her beloved's face with a straight razor. He shuddered and looked away.

Mindy giggled. "Oh, my word, you're scared!"

"Of course I'm scared. If you're not scared, there's something wrong with you." Their eyes locked, and the smile slowly slid off her face. Had he gone too far? Had that been *too* sassy? No, he didn't think so. She wasn't glaring at him so much as *gazing* at him. *Don't even think it*, he told himself. *This is Mindy Rose. She's not going to be into some random civil engineer in the middle of nowhere.* And yet she was looking at him like a woman looks at a man when she's thinking those thoughts.

With great effort he pulled his eyes away from hers and tried to focus on the movie. But not long after, her hand brushed his in the popcorn bowl, and he could have sworn it was on purpose.

Chapter 15

M indy showered and then put on one of the new outfits Dustin
had bought for her. For a dude, he had pretty good taste. She
was trying to psych herself up. Keely would be there soon, and Mindy
would be able to go home, check in with her mother, and figure out
how she was going to handle this career crisis. This was all good news.
It should have been a relief. But she wasn't feeling happy or relieved.

She was sad. Sad about leaving Dustin.

Which was preposterous. She didn't even know him. Why did she
have such intense feelings for this guy? She tried to convince herself
that the feelings were a result of the crisis. *For the first time in a
long time, you are living in real America. You are experiencing the
small-town life you love with real, salt-of-the-earth people, and this is
making you happy. It's not really about Dustin. You just want this way
of life.* This made sense, and she tried to believe it, but it was a struggle.

There was just something about Dustin Honeywood. She hadn't felt like this about a man since ... well, since her first love had broken her heart in the ninth grade.

It had been a while.

She left her room and was sad to find out that Dustin had left the ranch. Of course he had. She'd been stupid to think that he'd be there. It was Monday. Real people, salt-of-the-earth people, had jobs and schedules and commitments. If she'd wanted to see him, she shouldn't have slept so late.

She gave the house a once over to make sure Chase wasn't lurking somewhere. He wasn't. Good. She wanted to have the house to herself so she could talk straight with Keely and not be overheard. She used the landline to call her best friend and see where she was at. She hoped she was this side of the Missouri.

"Hey, I'm so glad you called." Oh no. Keely sounded worried. "I have a small problem."

Mindy already knew that whatever the problem was, it wasn't small. "What's wrong?"

"I'm in Arkansas."

Mindy's heart sank. "Are you okay?"

"Yes, I'm fine," she said quickly. "But my car is in the shop. They say they won't even be able to look at it until tomorrow. I tried to look for a different mechanic, but ... I'm in *Arkansas*."

Mindy laughed. "Where in Arkansas?"

"Ozark Acres."

Mindy tried to place it.

"I know. It sounds like a retirement home, but I guess it's a town. Sort of. It's incredibly beautiful, so I've got that going for me. That doesn't help you much, though."

Mindy still didn't know where she was exactly. "Is that on a highway?"

"No, Min, there *is* no highway that goes from Alabama to middle of nowhere South Dakota."

"Oh. Sorry." She felt like she'd traveled every road in the country, but she hadn't navigated any. She sighed. "Okay, well, are you safe? I mean, should I send help?"

"Won't that give away your location?"

"Maybe. I don't know, Keely. Maybe it's time to do that anyway. I probably should get back to it." The idea made her feel ill. "It's not like I can hide out forever."

"But, Mindy, can't you? I mean, I know you have done a great job taking care of your mom, but don't you have enough money socked away so you can keep doing that even without all the rhinestones?"

Mindy sighed. "I might, but it would be tight, and I don't want to come up short. I'm not as rich as people think I am, Keely. My contract kind of stinks. I probably shouldn't have signed it, but I was young and stupid."

"You're still young."

"And hopefully not as stupid."

Keely laughed. "You were never stupid. Stop being so hard on yourself. You have worked your tail off, and when the opportunity came for you to get to the next level, you took it. I doubt most people get a great contract in the beginning. They didn't know you were going to take off like you did, or they would've given you a better one."

"Thanks, Keely. You always make me feel better."

"How much longer is your contract?"

"Five years."

Keely didn't say anything.

"I'm not gonna survive another five years, Keely." Her voice cracked. She took a deep breath and tried to regain control. She had no problem crying in front of Keely. She'd done it at least a thousand times. But Chase could pop up at any second. "I can do it. I just ..." She didn't know if she could. But she knew that she needed to. "I mean, I knew I wasn't happy, but I didn't care. It's not about me or my happiness. But then, Keely, I really *lost* it. Like I lost control of myself. I can call my manager and be picked up in a few hours, but what if that happens again? I don't know how to keep it from happening again."

"That's actually a really good question, my friend, and I wouldn't even consider going back until you have an answer." She paused. "Min, you never told me what *caused* your panic attack."

"I don't really know."

"You've never held out on me before."

"I'm not holding out. At least not on purpose. I don't understand it. I guess that's scaring me too, the fact that I can't even understand my own behavior."

"Well, what happened right before you tweaked?"

Mindy smiled at her use of the word *tweaked*. She closed her eyes and thought back. "Nothing different. In fact, I wasn't even as stressed as usual, except that I didn't want to wear that stupid dress. But I was happy to be doing an outdoor show, and I was happy that the stage was smaller."

"Why does the size of the stage matter?"

Mindy sighed. "It doesn't. Not really. I was just being weird, and at the time, I was thinking that a small stage was more like the old days when shows were more ... I don't know the word I'm looking for."

"Intimate?" Keely guessed.

"*Real.*"

"Oh. That makes sense."

"So I was happy to be so close to the fans, and they were super great. They knew my songs, and they loved me, and I appreciated them, but then ... I don't know. The lights were really bright. Like I was blinded, and then I couldn't breathe, and the stupid dress was too tight."

"Why did you have to wear a particular dress?"

"I don't know. They pick out my clothes."

"Why didn't you like it?"

"It was hideous. And it was too tight. And I was practically naked."

"Yeah, I know you've mentioned before that they try to save on fabric."

Mindy snickered. "Yeah, that must be it."

"Sounds to me like it was the dress."

"I'm not going to blame a dress for a mental breakdown."

"Why not? It was the straw that broke your back. How much sleep have you been getting?"

"I never sleep. Well, actually, I've been sleeping like an old dog for the last few days, but before I got here ... I can't remember the last time I slept for more than a few hours at a time."

"And have you been eating healthy?"

"I hadn't been eating at all. I had to lose a few pounds, but I really didn't have any appetite."

"Mindy, you have *never* needed to lose a few pounds."

"Yeah, well, that's not what my manager said."

"I hate your manager."

Mindy laughed. She loved her friend so much. "Don't hate him. Hating him will hurt you, not him."

"I hate him," she insisted. "Anyway, so you were stressed out, malnourished, sleep deprived, and you couldn't breathe because your dress was too tight. I think we figured it out."

"It was more than that."

"Tell me."

"It's the whole thing. It's the job. I'm singing songs I don't want to sing and acting like someone I don't want to be."

"And wearing things you don't want to wear," Keely added.

"Yeah. But I don't want to sound like a brat. I mean, I have my dream job. I have the job that thousands and thousands of people want. What is my problem?"

"You're acting. Round the clock acting. And that's exhausting."

She sighed. "Yeah, maybe."

"Oh my goodness," Keely said all of a sudden. "Are you still wearing that *dress*?"

Mindy laughed. "No."

"Oh phew. I just pictured you sleeping in it and hanging out on a ranch in it. Scared me to death."

"No, no. I have clothes."

"Where did you get clothes? Did you rob a Walmart?"

"Not yet. First, some angel stripped down right in the street and gave me her dress so that I could blend into the crowd."

"What? That's awesome! Talk about a super-fan."

"I don't even think she *was* a fan. She wasn't at the show. She was hanging out at some outdoor bar. But somehow she read the scene and knew I needed help. Once I get this sorted, I'm going to try to find her so I can thank her."

"The great American hunt for the dress lady. Nice. I'm here for that."

Mindy laughed. "So I wore that for a long time, and then Dustin went and got me some clothes."

"Dustin?" She sounded far more intrigued than she should have been. "Is he the rancher?"

"Sort of. It's kind of a long story."

"Spill it. Right now."

She heard a noise in the back yard. "I can't right now. I hear his brother coming, and—"

"He has a *brother*?" she screeched. "Are all these people single?"

She laughed. "Yeah, but—"

"I'm going to start walking."

The door didn't open, but Mindy knew she'd heard something. "Don't do that. Okay, I've got to let you go for now, but are you sure you're all set? You don't need money?"

"I don't."

"And you're safe? You don't have to sleep in the woods or anything?"

"Nope. There is one motel. And it's not bad."

"Okay. Hey, you can call this number if anything changes."

"Okay, I will. And I'll try to get back on the road tomorrow. You have fun with your two brothers."

"There are six of them."

"Six?" she cried. "What is happening—"

"Gotta go, Keely. I love you. Bye!" She hung up and concentrated on listening, but all was quiet. She got up and looked out the window. She didn't see anyone, but she knew she'd heard something.

And Dustin's truck was in the driveway.

Chapter 16

Dustin knew it was wrong to eavesdrop, but he did it anyway. "I'm not gonna survive another five years, Keely." Mindy sounded like she was on the verge of tears.

His heart broke for her. She was too good for this. She was so talented, so beautiful. He knew that she would be a big star even if they let her be herself. She might even be a *bigger* star.

He realized Chase was standing fifty feet away, watching him. He headed that way.

"That's not creepy or anything," Chase said.

"Yeah." He had no defense.

"What were you listening for?"

"I wasn't listening for anything, but then I heard her talking on the phone, and yeah, I might have eavesdropped a little."

"Why are you here?"

The truth was embarrassing, but if he didn't tell it, then Chase's imagination would come up with something worse. "There's an older

woman in town and while I was working on the water line, I accidentally messed up her garden—"

Chase's eyes traveled to where Dustin had been standing. "So you
came to steal our *poppies*?" He made it sound so terrible.

"Not all of them. Just a few. You wouldn't even have noticed they
were gone."

"I would have noticed."

"Chase, she's a sweet woman. And I killed her flowers."

Chase growled. "Fine. Dig up my poppies. But leave the yellow
ones."

Dustin found this prescription odd and amusing, but he didn't
comment. He went back to get the poppies, and when he did, he heard
Mindy say his name. His ears perked up. "… kind of a long story," she
said. What? What did that mean? He held his breath and listened, but
she said she heard someone coming, and her voice got a lot quieter.
Dustin busied himself with the poppies.

He was just about done when she came around the corner of the
house and let out a little screech. "Why are you kneeling in the dirt?"

He looked up at her, and the sun was directly behind her head,
making her look like an angel. "Seriously? Isn't it obvious?"

She looked down. "Oh. I didn't see the flowers."

"Yeah, there are flowers. What did you think I was doing?" *Whoa,
easy, man. Don't protest too much.*

"I didn't know! That's why I asked! Why are you digging up flowers
in the middle of the day?"

Dustin didn't fear Chase's imagination as much as he did hers. "It's
for work."

"Aren't you an engineer?"

He stood up and brushed his hands off. "Yes." He tried to look dignified as he bent to pick up his confiscated poppies. When he straightened back up, holding his tray of flowers, she was looking at the window.

"Did you, uh, hear anything?" The degree of her worry made him feel bad.

"I heard you talking, but I didn't hear anything of note."

She relaxed. "Oh. Okay. So ... uh ..." She looked at the flowers. "Are you going to go now?"

"Yeah. I need to get back."

"Okay." She started toward his truck, and he fell into step beside her.

"So that was the friend who is coming to get me. But her car broke down in Arkansas."

"Oh." He tried to hide the fact that this was great news.

"Yeah."

"Is she okay? Has someone helped her?"

"Yes to both questions. She's got a motel and a mechanic, but she's obviously not going to get here today."

"Okay."

They reached the truck, and she turned toward him. "I can ask Hudson when he gets home. I don't want to bother Chase. But do you think it would be okay if I stayed another night?"

"I *know* it would be okay."

"Yeah?"

"Yeah."

"Okay." Her smile was so sweet and innocent. "Thanks, then. Have a good rest of your day."

"You too." He got into the truck and wondered what it meant that she stood there watching him drive away. So now he sort of knew why she'd run off stage. She didn't have a crazed super-fan after her after all. In a way the truth was worse than that, or at least more complicated. She was burned out. And her people were making her do things that made her uncomfortable. This made him angry. He had to figure out a way to help her.

Chapter 17

After Dustin absconded with his abducted poppies, Mindy returned to the back yard and got down on her hands and knees to weed around the remaining flowers. It was still early summer, so there weren't many weeds, and she didn't have a whole lot else on her calendar that day, so she took her time.

She had decided to weed because she was bored and felt guilty sitting around doing nothing. She hadn't expected the weeding to have an effect on her, but it was. First, the scent of the earth was strong and intoxicating. She'd spent most of her childhood playing outside, getting dirty, but she couldn't remember ever loving the smell of soil. But now she did. It smelled fresh and clean and powerful, and sinking her fingers into it to dig out roots was oddly satisfying. The soil was cool and refreshing, as was the slight breeze that tickled the back of her neck as it blew her thin layer of sweat dry.

She saw Chase watching and was grateful he couldn't hear her thoughts. He would think she was raving mad.

Despite taking her time, the whole flower bed was fully weeded in an hour. She scanned the property for another garden but didn't see any. She went around to the front of the house and found another small flower bed. This excited her, and she weeded that too.

When she couldn't find another weed to pull, she stood up and stretched her back. Chase was leading a horse into the barn. She figured he was doing the evening chores, and she also figured that she should help, even though she was nervous about approaching him.

"I ran out of weeds," she said when she got close. She shoved her hands in her back pockets.

"Yeah."

Wow, a man of many words.

"Can I help with anything?"

He looked at the flower bed and then at her. It seemed he didn't understand the question.

"Can I help with chores? I know how to clean out a stall." She grinned.

He looked surprised. "You do?"

"Yeah. We have horses in Alabama." She'd never had any herself, but she'd been around plenty.

"I got it. Thanks."

"Okay. I'll find something that needs doing." She went into the barn. She hadn't been in this one before, and it was newer and much more modern than the one she'd hidden in. It had more stalls than horses, and she could feel the Honeywood brothers' dream of filling the rest of the space. She found a broom and started sweeping but soon got distracted by a gorgeous chestnut horse who stuck its head over the stall door to watch her. "Well, hello," she said softly. "Who are you, gorgeous?" She calmly approached, not wanting to startle it. She held her arm out, offering the back of her hand to its nose. "There, see? We can be friends. I could sure use a friend." She gently ran her hand down the horse's neck. "How about you?" She stepped closer, still stroking its silky hair. "I mean, I know you have Chase, but would you like to have another friend?" She brought her face closer to its face, and it perked its ears forward and nickered softly. Mindy giggled. "Why, thank you. I appreciate that. Aren't you a friendly little thing?" Although it wasn't that little. "What's your name, beautiful?"

Of course, it didn't answer. It did, however, swing its head toward her, and she giggled with delight and ran her hand down its nose. "I'm Mindy," she whispered, "but don't tell anyone. That can be our little secret." She wished she could go for a ride. It had been too long. But she wasn't about to ask Chase for a favor like that. She vowed that when she got back to her real life, she would make time to go for a ride. Part of her knew this probably wouldn't happen, not until her tour was over anyway, but still—it was a nice thought. It gave her hope. Maybe she could suggest horses for her next video.

Chapter 18

C hase watched their guest from the far end of the barn. At first he was annoyed that she was approaching the horse, but then when he saw the way she did so, he changed his mind.

She was obviously a horse lover. And he noticed something else too. She was relating to that mare a lot differently than he'd seen her relate to any human so far. He could understand that. The woman's shoulders were relaxed, and her smile was different, more sincere, more vulnerable. Even her voice had changed tone.

No one put on airs for a horse. So if this was the real woman, then who was she trying to be in the house? And why the act? Was she afraid to be herself? Or was she just so uncomfortable that she couldn't allow herself to be who she was?

Chase knew what it was like to be a fish out of water, to be so worried about the next blow landing that he had to walk around stiff and alert, to be so worried about the world running out of air that it was hard to breathe. And when Chase was around horses, it was like that fish getting back into the water. All his muscles relaxed. His *soul* relaxed. He was safe. He was himself.

Maybe this woman lived a life similar to his. This thought brought an unexpected, and rather unwelcome, flood of sympathy.

He cleared his throat and approached.

She looked up quickly, but she didn't jump. "Hope it's okay," she said softly. "It's just so beautiful that I couldn't not touch it."

Chase nodded. "She is a beauty, and I named her Hope. Hope, this is Mandy."

The woman stiffened. Yep, a fish out of water. "What kind of horse is she?"

"Hanoverian."

"Oh wow." She leaned a little closer to Hope. "You *are* special. I had a feelin'."

They stood in silence for a moment, each enjoying Hope's presence.

"And that's a great name," she said without looking at him.

"Thank you. Know why I named her Hope?" Of course she didn't know, but as he'd expected, she was all ears.

"Because God is always in control, so that means there is always hope." He reached out and ran his hand down Hope's neck. "No matter how I'm feeling or what I'm scared of on a given day, no matter how confused I am or how out of place I feel in this world, there is still hope." He stopped talking. He was exhausted. But he'd wanted to let her know that she wasn't alone in whatever she was going through, and he wanted to do it without making her think there were two Honeywood brothers after her.

He took a step back. "Would you like to ride her?"

Her eyes grew wide. "Are you serious?"

Of course he was serious. As if he'd tease her with an offer like that. He stared at her.

"And obviously she's a good riding horse, safe and all that?"

"She's perfect."

"Then I would love that." She looked like she might burst into tears.

He really didn't want that to happen. "All right." He looked at the time. "Give me a few minutes, and I'll have her ready for you." He went into the tack room, which had sort of become his backup living quarters. It was so nice he was thinking about moving out here for good, but he didn't want to hurt Hudson's feelings. Although, if his brothers kept bringing stray women here, he might do it anyway. He dialed Dustin's number. "Hurry up and get here, man. You need to go for a horseback ride with your girlfriend."

"I'm still at work, and she's not my girlfriend."

"Not yet, maybe."

Dustin didn't say anything.

"You going to come ride with her?"

"She wants to?"

"She's champing at the bit."

"Okay. I'll be right there."

"Good." Chase started to hang up.

"What are you going to be doing?"

"I don't know. Sitting around twiddling my thumbs waiting for some random woman to need to hole up at this ranch."

Dustin laughed. "What?"

"You know, I figured it must be my turn by now." He hung up before Dustin could say anything else. He'd been kidding, of course, but it was fun to leave Dustin wondering.

Chapter 19

Mindy stood there for so long with the beautiful Hope that she was starting to think Chase had forgotten about her and wasn't coming back. It had to be gaining on supper time.

At first she'd been glad he'd left her alone because something about what he'd said, or maybe it was the matter-of-fact way he'd said it, had made her very emotional. She'd stood there for a minute just crying with the horse. And the horse hadn't seemed to mind. In fact, as insane as it was, it almost seemed that the horse understood. Of course, this was Chase's horse, so maybe she did. "Yeah, you're an emotionally intelligent being, aren't you?" Mindy had said, and then she'd pulled herself together, expecting Chase's imminent return.

Was this weird, her going on a ride with him? It didn't feel weird, but she did like Dustin, and she didn't want to make him jealous or hurt his feelings. And she didn't think they had any real chance of turning into a thing, but even if it was one in a million, she didn't want to make her odds even worse by making him think she had a thing for Chase. She winced. She felt bad for the woman that would eventually take on that challenge. That woman would have to be an emotional powerhouse.

Just when she was about to give up, say goodbye to Hope, and head inside, she heard a voice.

No, not a voice. Voices, plural. Why was there more than one?

Chase walked into the barn with Dustin in tow, and neither of them acted like this was odd. Chase immediately busied himself saddling a different horse, and Dustin smiled at her and then opened the stall door to get Hope.

"Would you like to do the honors?" Dustin said.

She didn't know what he meant, and he pointed his chin at a nearby saddle.

Mindy thought she could probably safely saddle Hope, but it had been forever, and she didn't want to get back on that bicycle in front of these two. "No, thank you."

Unfazed by her no, he quickly and smoothly got Hope ready and then led her out of the barn. Mindy followed. Once they were out in the light, Dustin offered her a hand. She wasn't sure she needed it, but again, she didn't want to fail in front of these two, so she accepted his help, and then she was on Hope's back, and she felt like she was flying.

Hope was rock steady beneath her, and she ran a hand down her neck. "Wow, girl, you sure are making me feel better. Thanks for that. I owe you one." Great. Now she was getting attached to *two* souls here at the Honeywood Ranch. She was never going to be able to leave.

And she kind of wished she didn't have to. She could move her mom out to South Dakota, and they could start over.

She shook her head. No. That was ridiculous. She had obligations to fulfill and money to earn. She exhaled slowly. This was just a brief reprieve, and then she was going back to work. Somehow.

Before she realized what was happening, Dustin was sitting alongside her on his own horse, and Chase was nowhere in sight.

"Isn't Chase coming?"

"Oh no, he said he's got too much work to do."

Was this a set up? Had Chase played matchmaker? Or was he just trying to get rid of her?

"Don't worry, this isn't a set up." Wow, what a mind reader. "My guess is that Chase sensed you really needed a ride, so he just told me to chaperone." He reached down and patted his horse's neck. "Chase says you've done this before?"

"I have ... but I'm not sure I told *him* that?"

Dustin shrugged. "Chase just knows things. All right, do you have a particular direction you'd like to go?"

She shook her head. "It's your home field, so you decide."

"Okay. Chase has worn a path along the creek. Let's go there." He clicked his tongue, and they were off. She got the impression that the click had been more to let her know he was moving than it had been for the horse. It seemed the horse would have gone without it. A little nervous, she gently squeezed Hope with her legs, and Hope started walking.

Mindy was on top of the world. This was way better than being on stage. This was freedom. This was living. Of course, she might like being on stage more if they'd let her sing songs about horses. "I wish

I was a songwriter so—" She broke off, horrified that she'd said the words aloud. Her face caught fire, and she started to sweat all over.

Dustin turned and looked back at her. "You wish you were a songwriter, so what?"

So that I could write my own songs, she couldn't say. "So that I could try and capture feelings as good as this," she said instead.

"That's a pretty poetic statement. Maybe you are a songwriter and just don't know it yet. Maybe you just need a few days off from the grind every once in a while."

"The grind?" she said suspiciously. "What makes you think I have a grind?"

He looked away. "Doesn't every working American have a grind?"

Oh. He'd meant the waitressing grind. She needed to be less suspicious. "Oh, yeah. I guess maybe that would help." But she knew she still wouldn't be able to write songs.

"Have you ever tried?"

"To write songs?"

"Yeah."

She sure had. She'd tried a lot. And she'd failed a lot. But she didn't want to tell him that. She also didn't want to lie. It was one thing to leave things out. It was another thing entirely to make things up. "Not hard enough, I guess."

He chuckled. "But you've got good ideas. Maybe you just need a writing partner."

They reached the brook and started following it. "What makes you think I've got good ideas?" The sun was sinking toward the horizon, bathing the whole world in an orange palette of infinite shades. She couldn't remember being so happy.

"You just told me one. Was that the first good idea you've ever had?" He said this teasingly.

"I don't know. Maybe. I don't usually say them out loud."

"Well, maybe you should. Maybe that's what's missing."

She stared at him. His words were hitting a little too close to home. Did he know more than he was letting on? She decided to ignore him and focus on Hope, focus on her rhythm, on how being in that saddle almost felt like dancing. And the kind of dancing that hadn't been choreographed months in advance by a team of men trained in marketing. Real dancing. The dancing people did with feeling.

They rode in silence for some time, and she started to feel guilty for ignoring him. "So your job, do you like it?"

He shrugged. "I just wanted a steady gig, and it's steady, all right. People need water."

"I suppose that's true. Did you go to college for engineering?"

"Yes, ma'am. South Dakota State."

"Wow, you Honeywood boys sure do stay close to home."

He laughed. "Not all of us. Chase was gone for years, and Burke is constantly on the road."

"Oh yeah. That's the rodeo brother, right?"

"That's right." He shook his head. "Burke is kind of crazy." Then he laughed. "But we love him, so we keep him."

"And I think I heard someone say that he is married?"

"Yep. He and Ava have always been inseparable. High school sweethearts. He's the only one of us who is married, but I expect Wyatt will be getting hitched soon."

"Maybe they can be the venue's first clients."

He laughed again. "First and only clients."

Silence took over again, and she tried to think of another question she could ask him—one that wouldn't prompt him to turn the question back on her. She couldn't say, "What do you do for fun?" because then he might ask her the same thing and she would have to say, "rehearsal" or "watch *New Girl* reruns on my tour bus."

"I like Olivia. She was so kind to me, and she made me laugh."

"Yeah, she's a keeper. Oh man, when she first moved here, she accidentally ran into us at church, and she acted like such a nut. She actually tried to crawl—well, no, it was more like duck walk—out of the sanctuary. I couldn't believe it. You know how you're like super awkward when you're fourteen and around the opposite sex?" He glanced at her. "Well maybe you weren't, but I sure was. Anyway, that's how she was acting, like she was at a junior high dance, but she's a grown woman. So anyway, I felt so bad for her, so I got right down there with her. I squatted right down to help. And I thought it was hysterical, but you know what? Most of the people around us didn't even give me a second look, and literally no one mentioned it afterward. So maybe I'm always that weird and I just don't usually notice, but that time I was doing it on purpose."

"You're not weird," she said quickly. "You just have the ability to be silly. That's a good thing for an adult to have." She wished she had more of it. And she had until recently. Maybe that would help her mental health if she could get some of her silly back. Maybe she should go duck walk around a church sanctuary.

"I don't know about silly, but I do like to laugh."

"I can't picture you being awkward, even as a fourteen-year-old."

"Oh no? Do I seem super suave to you?"

She snickered. "Not when you say things like *super suave*."

The creek and their path curved back toward the road and away from the setting sun, which made her sad, but the scenery was still breathtaking. She tried to think of another question to ask him. She liked to hear him talk. And it was even better when that talking made her laugh. But she couldn't think of anything.

Chapter 20

D ustin had to work to keep his eyes off the woman riding Hope. He'd never seen her so beautiful, and she was always beautiful.

He tried to think of something nice to say. He wanted to make her feel good, to make her feel special without freaking her out. "You look like a natural on that horse."

She giggled. "Hardly."

"No, you do. You look comfortable, confident. That's not common."

"Oh yeah? You go horseback riding with a lot of women?"

"A few, yeah."

Something like jealousy sparked on her face and then disappeared.

It was hard to compliment a woman he was supposed to know nothing about. All the nice things he wanted to say, all the *true* things, would all reveal that he knew more about her than she thought he knew.

He was growing increasingly worried about that. The longer she was at the ranch, the more time he spent with her, the more it felt like an actual lie. Of course he knew who she was. Everyone in the country did, except, apparently, his weirdo brothers. He was glad Burke wasn't here. Burke would be having a fit. That dude really loved his country music.

"I saw what you did with the flower bed. Thanks for that."

"Yeah, you're welcome. I had to do something after someone butchered it."

He chuckled. "I didn't butcher it."

"Okay, but really. Why did you steal poppies?"

He explained it to her as quickly as possible. It wasn't his favorite story to tell.

"Wow, that's pretty sweet of you, looking out for a senior's feelings like that."

"You would have done the same thing."

"How could you possibly know that?"

He shrugged. "I might not be able to read people as well as Chase, but I am a pretty good judge of character."

"Good to know." Her tone suggested that this wasn't a good thing at all. She was probably worried that he could intuit that she was lying. If she only knew. He didn't need his intuition for that.

"So do you like living in West Hope?" she asked.

"I do. It's not perfect, but nowhere is. And I can't imagine anywhere better."

"Have you always felt that way?"

"Pretty much. I know some kids grow up itching to get away, but I was never like that. I had such an easy childhood. I had good friends, didn't get picked on, good parents, good church, good school ... I didn't have anything to want to get away from."

"I don't think kids like that are always trying to get *away* from something," she said. "But the world sort of pushes ideas that the bigger and better is out there somewhere, always somewhere other than home. It's too bad because if home is where your family and friends are, then home keeps you safe and strong."

He glanced over at her, and the setting sun made her hair shine like pure gold. "You're pretty smart, aren't you?"

"Not really. I told you that I failed high school geometry."

He chuckled. "I don't think high school geometry is a reliable indicator of intelligence."

"Either way, I don't feel very smart very often."

This made his chest ache. "Well, you should because you are." He wished he could have more time with her. He didn't think he could convince her by morning.

They were quiet for a few minutes until she asked, "So have you ridden horses your whole life?"

"Not really. Chase was involved with a local ranch and with 4H, so he rode a lot, but I only got to once in a while. I'm still not as comfortable as I'd like to be."

"But it's pretty awesome, isn't it?"

He stared at her, completely smitten. "Yeah, it sure is."

Chapter 21

Why isn't he asking me anything about myself? Mindy wondered. She was working way harder at this conversation than he was.

Maybe he'd noticed how private she'd been, and he was respecting her boundaries.

If so, he was respecting them *a lot.*

She was insulted that he wasn't showing any interest in her, but this was silly. If he *did* show interest in her, it would cause problems. She would have to lie, and she didn't want to lie.

So stop wishing he'd ask you questions.

Wait. Maybe that was *why* he wasn't asking her about herself. Maybe he knew she would have to lie, and he didn't want to hear it.

She grew suspicious again. She'd been at the ranch for three days, and he'd hardly asked anything about her. That was weird. Wasn't it? She looked at him, seeing him in a whole new light.

He knows who you are.

The theory struck pain in her heart, but it explained everything: why he hadn't asked her anything, why he hadn't pressed her to report the pretend friends to the sheriff, why he'd been so helpful, and why he'd interrupted Hudson when Hudson had been interrogating her about waitressing.

That was how a person acted when they met someone new—the way Hudson had been acting.

Not the way Dustin had been acting.

Dustin had been acting like he already knew her.

She was such an idiot. How could she not have seen it? Dustin had known all along.

Her brain searched for a way to poke holes in this theory, but she knew it was more than a theory. So then why had he been hiding it? Why let her keep up her ruse?

And then she remembered the distinct discordant sound of his awful rendition of the John Anderson tune. And the fact that he'd been in Deadwood with his own guitar. He hadn't been at her concert. He'd been playing somewhere. This guy wanted to be a musician. Or a singer. So he'd been going along with her act so that he could use her to get to where he wanted to go.

Growing angrier by the second, she glared at him, and as she did, she saw something behind her. Instinctively, she pulled up on her reins. Hope stopped on a dime. "Dustin," Mindy whispered.

Dustin's eyes followed hers to the car parked on the side of the road with its hood up.

She was out in the open. On horseback. Totally exposed with nowhere to hide.

Dustin looked at the car, looked at her, and looked back at the car again—contemplating. He gave her an apologetic look. "They're obviously having trouble. I'm sorry. I can't not help them. Can you wait here?"

She nodded. Yep, he definitely knew. He hadn't said, "Want to go help them?" or "Let's go help them." He'd asked her to wait there, at a distance.

He knew.

She turned Hope around and created some more distance between herself and the car. If they were going to look up and see her, they were going to see her back and the horse's tail.

Unless they've already seen you.

Which they well might have. She'd been so busy glaring at the gorgeous engineer, she'd forgotten she was supposed to be on alert. She had forgotten that there was a road right there that connected them to the rest of the world. She'd forgotten that other people lived in this world, people besides her and Dustin Honeywood.

She waited a long time without looking back, but then she couldn't stand it anymore. He was taking forever, so she turned to see what was happening, and one of those other people in the world had a phone held up and pointed at her. She turned away quickly, panic running through her.

Just a coincidence, she told herself. He was photographing the scenery. Even if he'd recognized her, he wouldn't be taking pictures of her back. It was just a coincidence.

Chapter 22

One of the stranded people was a teenage girl, and Dustin kept a closer eye on her as he tried to figure out what was wrong with their car. She kept staring in Mindy's direction, though Mindy was so far away, Dustin didn't see how the kid could recognize her.

But then he caught her taking pictures. "Any reason you're taking pictures of my girlfriend?" The lie was unintentional. He'd been in such a hurry to speak that his brain had just come up with the most efficient way to get the message out: *Stop filming my woman.*

The girl didn't spare him a glance and sure didn't lower her phone. "She's your girlfriend? No way!"

His stomach sank. That comment could only mean one thing, right? But he wanted to make sure. "Why is that so hard to believe?"

She turned and looked at him curiously. Then she shrugged and tucked the phone in her pocket.

Dustin didn't know how to interpret this. If she'd recognized Mindy, surely she would have said something? Surely she would have suggested that Mindy wasn't really his girlfriend? She would have been right.

Dustin hurriedly finished what he was doing and then closed the hood. "You guys should be okay to get to town, but then you need to get it to a shop. I can recommend someone?" He gave them Rodney's info. Then he tipped his hat, said, "Have a good evening," and got on his horse.

None of them thanked him, which irked him, but he tried not to let it.

Mindy started riding away before he caught up to her. Under other circumstances he would have been offended, but he understood. Maybe he should have sent her back toward the house before he'd left her. He'd thought she was far enough away to look like any other blonde. He tried to convince himself that he'd been right.

When they were well out of sight, she leveled a gaze at him. "Why were they taking pictures of me?"

How was he supposed to answer that? He wished they could just have an honest conversation without pretending that she wasn't Mindy Rose. Maybe it was time for that. Maybe he should just come out with it. But then what? Would she run away? And where would she go?

He sighed. She was safest with him. He didn't want to push her away. "I asked, but she didn't answer me."

Mindy said nothing, but the lighthearted mood of their ride was completely trashed.

"Do you want to head back?" he asked.

"I guess we should," she said, sounding crestfallen.

Chase met them in the barn and offered to take care of the horses, but Dustin and Mindy said no. Chase hovered nearby, but he gave them their space.

When Dustin was finished tending his horse, Mindy was still grooming Hope. "It's therapeutic, isn't it?" he said.

She nodded, wiping her eyes with the back of her hand.

He longed to take her into his arms and comfort her, but he knew that would make things even more complicated than they were, so he tried to think of something else he could do, something he could say to make her feel better, or at least distract her. "I know we're a long way from Alabama, but I think Hope might like it if you would come back and visit sometime."

She leaned her forehead against the horse's side and then turned her face to look at him. "Maybe." It was clear that she didn't think that would happen.

He hated it, but he couldn't think of a way to encourage her, not without letting on that he knew her secret. "Do you need anything else? I'm going to head inside." He didn't want to leave her, but he thought Hope was doing more good for her than he could, and he didn't want to get in the way.

"I'm good." Her words were clipped. Was she angry? Was she angry with *him?*

"Okay, see you inside, then."

She didn't say anything more, and he walked back to the house with his head down. This was depressing. He really liked her, but he didn't even know her, and the woman she really was was really far out of his reach. This was really too bad because he would have liked her just as much if she wasn't rich and famous.

"Did you lose someone?" Hudson asked when Dustin got inside.

"No, she was reluctant to leave Hope." He went to the sink to wash his hands.

"Can't blame her there. Is Chase still out there?"

"Yeah, I think so."

Hudson raised an eyebrow, asking if Chase was trying to steal her away, but Dustin didn't have the energy to respond. No, no one was getting stolen. He had to have a chance with someone before she could be stolen away.

"Wasn't tonight the night you were going back to your place?" Hudson asked.

"Trying to get rid of me?" Dustin stuck his head in the fridge to grab a coke from the back. It was hard to reach them past all of Hudson's carrot juice.

"No, not at all. I just thought you said that the bug guy would be done by now."

"They did say that, yes. I plan to head home after supper."

Hudson glanced at the door. "Well, no one needs to know that they're done if you want to stick around a little while longer."

"Nah, that's okay." What was the point? And his back was sick of sleeping on a couch.

"Her friend is going to be here tomorrow, right?"

"Supposed to be."

"Sorry, man."

"I'll be okay," Dustin said. "Not the first crush I've ever had that didn't turn into anything." This was true. It wasn't his first fruitless crush. But it was the first one to sting this bad.

Chapter 23

When Mindy heard the news, she was surprised how sad it made her. Dustin was going home after supper? No one looked at her while they discussed it, and why would they? It had nothing to do with her. And yet, she felt left out. This was stupid, of course, because she was mad at him.

"What time is your friend getting here tomorrow?" Hudson asked.

"I'm not sure. I should call her soon and check in."

"Okay, well just know that she's welcome to crash here for a night if she wants to."

"Thank you. That's very kind." She didn't expect to take him up on the offer, especially not if there were new blurry photos of her floating around the Internet. It was high time to get out of Dodge.

Dustin offered to help with the dishes, but Hudson shooed him away. Dustin looked at her. "Walk me out?"

She nodded, happy that he'd asked. Why was it so hard to stay angry with him?

As they stepped down off the porch and into the darkness, awkwardness enveloped them, and they strode to the truck in silence. When they got there, he pressed a card into her palm. "Here's my number just in case you ever need it."

"Thank you," she said and meant it. Maybe they could keep in touch somehow. She didn't know what that would look like. Or maybe it was best to make a clean break. She was a little upset with him for trying to use her. *But he didn't even let you kiss him, so he can't be too much of a jerk.* She shook that thought out of her head. She didn't need to be having feelings for this guy. She had to get home, talk with her mother, and figure out what was next for her.

"I'm sorry this is so weird," she finally spit out. "I'm not trying to make things more awkward. I'm just not sure what to think about ... anything. My mind is all mixed up."

He smiled. "'Mixed Up Mind' would be a cool song title."

"What?" she snapped.

His smile faded. "Sorry. It was just that ... we were talking about song ideas ... before."

"Oh." *Girl, you can be a real jerk when you want to be.* She stood on her tiptoes and gave him a quick peck on the cheek, but when she pulled away, he grabbed her by both arms and pulled her in for a real kiss—and it *was* a real kiss. His passion took her breath away, and when he pulled away and let go, she staggered before she found her footing. "Whoa," she accidentally said out loud.

"It's been an honor to know you, Mindy. Have a safe trip." He got in his truck and started the engine without looking at her.

And only once she was watching him drive away did she realize what he'd just called her.

Mindy.

Or had she misheard?

Mindy sounded a lot like Mandy.

No, he'd said Mindy.

Had that been a slip of the tongue, or had he meant to say it? She looked down at the card in her hand.

Maybe she'd never know. Maybe it was better that way. Maybe she needed to stop analyzing a non-existent relationship with a man she was mad at.

She trudged back into the house.

Without looking at her, Hudson said, "My phone is on the table if you want to use it to check in with your friend."

"Oh, cool. Thank you." She found Keely's number and then took Hudson's phone outside.

"Hi," Keely said. In that one word, Mindy heard the bad news.

"Oh no."

"Yeah. They needed to order a part. I'm still in Arkansas."

"How much longer?"

"I don't know. They said the part should be here tomorrow, but they didn't make any promises."

Mindy felt sick. She took a deep breath. "Okay."

"I'm so sorry, Mindy."

"It's not your fault. Are you still okay money-wise?"

"Yeah. I'm good. It doesn't cost much to vacation in Ozark Acres, Arkansas."

Despite herself, Mindy laughed. "That's quite a mouthful."

"I know, but the place is really growing on me."

"Yeah." Mindy's eyes swept the moonlit vista in front of her. "I know the feeling."

Chapter 24

Dustin had been at work for less than an hour when Hudson started texting him. He was busy, so he ignored the first few texts, figuring he would get to them in a minute, but when Hudson called, Dustin figured something must up.

"Can you get over here?" Hudson said instead of a greeting.

"Why, what's up?"

"I don't really understand it. They're treating your girlfriend like a celebrity."

"She's not my—"

"But is she a celebrity?"

Dustin sighed. "Yeah, I'm afraid so."

"And you couldn't have mentioned that?"

"What is going on, Hudson?"

He groaned. "There are two TV vans here and some reporters, and every car that goes by stops and gawks. The yard is filling up fast."

Might be good publicity, Dustin thought. For the ranch, not so much for Mindy.

"If you don't get here quickly, I don't know if you'll be able to get close to the place. It's like Garth Brooks is in town."

Dustin laughed. That wasn't as much of a hyperbole as Hudson thought. "Let me get someone to cover for me, and then I'll be there."

"Can Seth cover for you?" Their youngest brother also worked for the water department, thanks to Dustin pulling some small-town strings.

"Maybe, but he's out on a call. Let me get off the phone so I can get there."

"Hurry. I'm not sure what to do here, and Chase is not much help."

This wasn't a surprise.

A half hour later Dustin saw the swarm of cars near his brothers' home. Oh boy. He'd known it would cause a ruckus, but he was surprised this many people cared. He drove off the road to get around the cars and cut across their land to get closer—and even then he couldn't get as close as he wanted.

He jumped out of his truck and searched the crowd for a familiar face. Were they all hiding inside? He weaved his way through the mob and went up onto the front steps.

"I wouldn't do that," a woman said, "Mr. Honeywood threatened to call the sheriff."

"I am Mr. Honeywood," Dustin grumbled, but he wasn't sure anyone heard him over the rumble of the crowd.

The front door was unlocked, which surprised him.

Mindy was sitting at the kitchen table, which surprised him even more. *Where did you expect to find her, cowering in the closet?*

"I'm so sorry," she said, her face wet with tears.

"Hey, it's okay." He went to her, and she pushed the chair back to get up. He took her into his arms and held her tightly. He kissed the top of her head. "What's your plan?"

She shook her head slightly. "Maybe saddle up Hope and head for the Black Hills? Worked for the bandits back in the day."

He chuckled. "That's a bad plan."

Hudson had entered the kitchen. "I don't know what to do here. They're like vultures."

Dustin looked out the window. "Have you guys said anything to them yet?"

"Not really," Hudson said. "I told them to get off my porch. I asked them to get off my land, but all they did was back up ten feet." He stepped closer to the window. "And it looks like they've undone that progress. I mean, I can call the sheriff, but"—he glanced at Mindy—"I wasn't sure what was going on, and I don't want to get her in trouble."

"Yeah, call him, would you?" Dustin let go of her and went out the door. "Hi, everybody. I'm Dustin Honeywood. This is my brother's ranch, and he's already asked you to leave. He's calling the sheriff right now, but we don't want any trouble or to cause anyone any trouble, so if you could all leave before they get here, that would be help—"

"Why is Mindy Rose here?" a man shouted.

"Mindy Rose is a wonderful person who deserves to have a little privacy when she needs it, and she would really appreciate it if you could all respect—"

"Why is she here?" another man shouted.

"None of your business!" Dustin shouted back, his short-lived diplomacy gone.

"Has she been here since Wild Bill Days?" someone shouted.

Dustin scanned the crowd, trying to find the asker.

"Is she sick?" "Is she on drugs?" "Did she have a breakdown?" "Is she in trouble?" "Is she pregnant?" "Are the rumors true?" "Is she quitting music?" "Who is she dating?" Their words melded together into an obnoxious cacophony. Was this what Mindy's life was like? This many voices? This many demands?

No wonder she'd jumped off the stage.

Chapter 25

Mindy crept to the window, careful to keep the curtain between her and the crowd.

"Mindy Rose is a wonderful person who deserves to have a little privacy."

She didn't deserve words that kind. She'd done nothing but lie and take Dustin for granted since she'd hidden in his truck.

They fired a dozen questions at him all at once. He tried to tell them it was none of their business, but that only spurred them on.

"No, she's perfectly healthy," Dustin said, answering a question she hadn't heard.

"She didn't look healthy when she was running down the Main Street of Deadwood," a woman said, and then several people chuckled.

Mindy ground her teeth together.

"Trust me," Dustin said, managing to sound completely trustworthy, "she had a reason to leave that concert in a hurry, but now she is fine."

"Does that mean that there was a threat? Was someone after her? Did someone—"

"Again, this is Ms. Rose's business, not yours. If and when she chooses to share her story, you'll get your answers then."

She smiled at him calling her Ms. Rose. Maybe she should fire her publicist. Actually, she thought dryly, her publicist had probably quit by now.

"Look, I know Mindy Rose is a phenomenally talented artist, and I know we all feel like we know her because we know her music so well, but the fact is that she is a person. She is her own person. And there are parts of her life we aren't going to know. This is one of those parts. Now, please, respect the person that she is by giving her some space right now."

She didn't hear anything, so after several seconds, she peeked around the curtain. The people in the yard were milling about, but they weren't leaving. It was as if they knew they had to move, but they couldn't quite decide where to go.

"Are they leaving?" Hudson whispered.

"Not yet."

"Hey, wait a minute," someone shouted.

It took Mindy a second to locate the speaker. He didn't look like a reporter. He was wearing a dirty tank top and swim trunks. He looked ridiculous. "I saw you that night. Is that how you know her? Because you're a country singer too?"

Dustin laughed. "No, no," he said emphatically.

The crowd started mumbling excitedly as if they'd just uncovered proof of something.

"I was there that night." Now he sounded irritated. "I was at an open mic. In South Dakota. Not Nashville. I am a civil engineer who can't carry a tune in a bucket. Now go home!" He didn't sound angry, but he sure sounded firm.

And they started to scatter—slowly. Some lingered, but most of them meandered toward the road.

When the door opened, she jumped back from the window like a spooked criminal.

Hudson laughed at her. "Good job, Dustin. Who knew you had such skills?"

Dustin chuckled. "I don't. I just talked to them." He looked exhausted.

"No, that was some advanced crowd control," Hudson said.

Mindy couldn't tell if he was being ironic. "Thank you," she said to Dustin.

"Of course. No big deal. I'm really sorry that they found out. I thought it would be safe to go for a horseback ride."

"It should have been," she said. "It's not your fault."

The three of them stood in an awkward triangle for a few seconds before Hudson wandered away. "I'm going to go check on Chase."

She looked at Dustin. "How long have you known?"

He gave her a crooked smile, and it was the sexiest smile she'd ever seen. He'd had a smile like that all along, and he'd been hiding it? "Darlin', I knew from the jump. You're a rock star."

Something about the way he said it melted her heart. He didn't sound star-struck; he sounded affectionate. He didn't say it in wonder;

he said it matter-of-factly. It was as if he'd known all along that she was famous; but all along, it hadn't factored into his thinking.

"I'm sorry I was mad at you. Seems pretty silly all of a sudden."

He let out a short, bewildered laugh. "You were mad at me?"

She looked at the floor. "I figured out that you knew. And so I wondered why you were pretending that you didn't. And well ... my theories didn't cast you in a good light." Her shame grew thicker. "I'm so sorry. You didn't deserve that. You've done nothing to indicate that you had bad intentions. I'm just used to ..."

He stepped closer. "Used to what?" he asked softly.

"No one ever just treats me like a person. Everybody always has an agenda."

"Oh, I had an agenda." That crooked smile threatened to make another appearance.

"Oh yeah? What's that?"

"To keep you safe, to give you time to recover from whatever was going on, and maybe get to know you a little."

Without permission her feet took her one step closer to him. Now his proximity was making her feel like she had a fever. "That was three agendas." She sounded a little breathless.

"Sorry. I had three agendas, I guess."

"Thank you for trying to help me." She sighed. "I have felt safe here, except for that time I almost got caught in the barn by the world's strangest wedding party."

"Oh, I bet the world's seen stranger."

She laughed. "Probably. Anyway, I appreciate you giving me space to ... recover. I wish I could just stay here forever."

"Why can't you?"

She laughed. Was he serious? "Have you enjoyed this circus? Because that's what it would always be like."

He shrugged. "I like circuses, but my point is, you don't need to be the great Mindy Rose." He put air quotes around her name, which she found adorable. "Can't you just be ... Mindy Rose? Like a normal woman with the life she wants, not the life her fans want? I mean I'm certainly not some expert in this stuff, but can't you just call off the show?"

Wow, he was so sweet. "I can't," she said softly.

"Why not?"

"My mom is sick. I've got her in a really great place, but it's not cheap."

It was clear he hadn't thought of that. "I'm sorry. I had no idea."

"I know."

"You said you had a sister, right?"

"I do. And she helps as much as she can, but she just doesn't make much money."

He sighed. It was really endearing how hard he was thinking about this. He shook his head. "There's just got to be a way that you can take care of your mother without torturing yourself."

"Maybe, but if there is, I sure haven't thought of it yet. Maybe you could help me brainstorm."

He smiled broadly. "Challenge accepted!" He elbowed her playfully and then made an exaggerated aw-shucks expression. "I'm kind of a problem solver. That's sort of my thing."

"Yeah, well, you are an engineer, so that makes sense." She wanted so badly to touch him but couldn't think of a way to make that happen naturally. She considered just leaping into his arms.

As if he sensed she was about to launch herself at him, he backed away. Then he turned, pushed the curtain out of the way, and peeked outside. "Hey! Most of them are gone!" He sounded surprised.

"Did you doubt your powers?"

"I sure did." He let go of the curtain and gestured toward the living room. "I do have to get back to work, but we could do a brainstorming session first?"

"Oh no," she said quickly. "I don't want to keep you from work. Hey, can I ask you a question?" She didn't know if it was the adrenaline or her feelings for Dustin, but something was emboldening her.

"Yeah, of course. Shoot."

All of her boldness fled—like air from a popped balloon. "You know what? Never mind."

He chuckled, studying her. "Don't do that to me. Are you trying to kill me with curiosity?"

She didn't know what to say.

"Come on, spit it out."

She wished she could rewind her life a few minutes. "I'm ... not sure how to phrase it."

His eyebrows went up. "Do you want me to guess?"

"Sure, that could be fun." She didn't want him to guess, but she was trying to buy herself an extra minute to come up with something.

He scratched his jaw and squinted. "You were going to ask me if I would be your new PR manager."

She laughed. "No! But that thought has crossed my mind."

"So then you were going to ask me to give you singing lessons."

She laughed again. "Actually, that could be fun too."

"Oh man, I just got this image of doing karaoke with you in town ..." Slowly his smile slid off his face. "But I guess you can't really be doing that kind of thing, can you?" He looked so sad that it broke her heart.

"You like me ..." she breathed. There. She'd said it.

He leveled a gaze at her, and it nearly melted her. "Was that a question? Or an observation?"

"A question."

He narrowed his eyes. "Of course I like you. You must know that. I don't go around kissing women I don't like."

That was good to know. "And you would like me if I wasn't a country music star." This one didn't sound like a question either, but it was supposed to.

"I think I'd like you *better* if you weren't—" He stopped, his eyes growing wide. "I'm sorry, I didn't mean that." He had no idea that he'd just said the one thing that would steal her heart forever. "I just meant that this would all be so much simpler. You know, we could—"

She couldn't stand it any longer. She threw her arms around his neck and planted a firm kiss on his lips. She ran a hand down his back and pulled his body closer. She didn't want to ever let go of this man again. And when he tried to pull away, she didn't let him. As the kiss grew more intense, she heard footsteps coming up from the basement and finally released him. "Go back to work," she whispered.

"Will you be here when I get back?"

She nodded. "I promise."

Chapter 26

Dustin had never been so distracted in his life. He tried to focus on his work, but it was a good thing he wasn't a bomb engineer.

He could not wait to get back to the ranch, back to Mindy. Was this what it was like? He'd always thought he would eventually fall madly in love and marry an awesome woman and have a family—but he'd never dreamed it would be such a powerful experience.

It was all-consuming.

He wanted to get on the road so bad that he was bouncing up and down. And then, when he managed to get into his truck, he had to concentrate to keep it near the speed limit.

But he made it to the ranch without getting arrested. He took a deep breath, hoping he didn't look as frantic as he felt, and stepped into the house. Mindy stood in the kitchen staring at him.

"Hi," she said stiffly.

"Hi," he said back.

Well, this was weird. They stood there staring at each other. He was so grateful that there were no brothers there to witness this. He would never hear the end of it.

"What's up?" he finally said.

"Oh nothing. Just didn't want to pummel you with my neediness as soon as you walked through the door. I thought I'd give you a minute to get settled in."

Interesting. He started toward her. "You're not needy, and I'm settled. What's up?"

She shrugged and tucked her hands into her pockets. It was difficult not to congratulate himself on his blue jeans selection. "I was just hoping we could have that brainstorming session."

"Oh, of course! Let me just grab a coke."

"See? I knew you weren't settled in yet."

"Do you want one?"

"Sure." She headed for the couch.

He followed her to the living room, focusing on not running. They settled in and looked at each other again. He really wanted to be looking at this face for the rest of his life. *Don't get ahead of yourself.* "Okay, give me the situation."

She took a big breath. "I love music more than I love anything, more than I love breathing. I am so, so grateful for my career, but I'm in this contract, and nearly everything about it is sucking the life out of me. But I can't quit because my mom needs to live where she living, which is expensive. Plus I don't even know if I want to quit because like I said, I love the music. And of course I don't want to disappoint the people who listen to my music. I care about them a great deal."

"Where is your mom?"

"She's in an assisted living facility, and it is a top-of-the-line place, man. She is treated like a queen. And I love it. I go see her as often as I can, and they never know I'm coming, and I never catch them being anything but awesome. And when I can't get there, I send Keely to spy. She sees the same thing. They are truly awesome." She looked at him. "She is so going to love you."

His heart leapt. That was a good sign. "I look forward to meeting her."

"When can you get time off from work?"

Ugh. He didn't have much vacation. "Not anytime soon, unfortunately."

"Okay, we'll solve that crisis next. Mine first." She laughed shrilly. "They're going to be here any second, by the way. I'm surprised they're not here yet.

"Who? Your manager?"

"Yes, and my publicist, and my drummer ... I've been watching the door worrying about who was going to come through it first."

"I won't let them through the door unless you want them through it."

She smiled, and light flashed in her eyes.

"Wait, your drummer? Why would they bring the drummer?"

"He's the closest thing I have to a real friend. They might bring him to try to talk some sense into me."

Something too much like jealousy burned in his chest.

"Don't worry. He's married with children. Not that you would worry. Not that you would be jealous." She groaned. "Ugh, stop talking, Mindy."

"No, don't. I like it when you talk. Okay, so he's your friend. So you probably know what he would say about this."

She scrunched up her face as she thought. "I think he'd say that I have my dream job and that I need to suck it up and get a better contract next time. He'd say, 'You signed up for this, Mindy.'"

"Wow, tough love."

She giggled lightly. "Is there any other kind?"

"Uh, yes, Mindy, there is." He was going to show her. "So is that a reasonable plan? Just dealing with it till the next contract?"

She slowly shook her head. "It sounds reasonable. I want it to be reasonable. But I didn't expect to have a meltdown on stage in Deadwood. So I don't really trust myself now. Just because something is reasonable doesn't mean I will be able to pull it off."

The house phone rang, and they both ignored it.

"I have an idea," Dustin said.

Her eyes lit up. "Yeah?"

"What would need to change for you to be okay? For you to trust yourself?"

She was still considering the question when Chase hollered up from the basement. "Hey, Queen of Country! It's for you!"

Chapter 27

M indy reached for the phone with a trembling hand. "Hello?

"You have a show in Reno tomorrow night. You'd better get on the road."

She exhaled shakily. She didn't know what to say.

"If you are not in Reno in time for rehearsal, your label will sue you for everything you've got and more. And they will make sure no other label will pick you up after they drop you."

She felt Dustin standing behind her before he laid a supportive hand on her shoulder. She doubted the label had that much power, and Vern must have sensed it. "Don't think your sweet and innocent act will protect you. They can make things up if they need to. Your record won't be so spotless when they're done."

She felt sick.

"Reno, Mindy."

"I—"

"I don't want to hear your excuses. This is your only option." Vern hung up. She put the phone in its cradle and then burst into tears. Dustin spun her around and took her into his arms. Vern hadn't even asked her what had happened. Which meant that he didn't care what had happened.

Dustin let her cry for a minute and then asked her who was on the phone.

"Vern. My manager."

"And what did Vern say?" He said his name as if it tasted sour.

She told him. He held her out at arms' length so he could smile down at her. She sniffed. "What could you possibly be smiling at?"

"You don't hate your job."

She wiped her eyes. "What are you talking about?"

"You love your job. At least most of it. So what would you need to change about it for you to be okay?"

She shook her head and sighed. She'd been sleeping better than she had in years, and she was still exhausted. She pulled away from him and went back to the couch. "I don't know how to answer that. I guess I want to sing better songs and not be forced to prance around half naked."

He gave her a moment and then asked, "Is that it?"

She tried to think of more aspects that needed to change, but she couldn't. This surprised her. How had something so complicated gotten so simple all of a sudden? "I don't know. I think so?"

He laughed. "Give it another minute. What else?"

But she truly couldn't think of anything else.

"Good. Then here's my brainstorm. You go to Reno, and you tell them that you don't want to have another panic attack and run off stage in the middle of a show ever again, but that you can't guarantee it won't happen again unless they make those few changes."

She felt her eyes grow wide. "I don't think I'm in any position to threaten them."

He shrugged. "It's not a threat. You are communicating your needs." He sat beside her and laid a warm hand on her knee. "Mindy, something significant happened in Deadwood. It's not like you just made it up. So you've got some ground to stand on here. Tell them you had a panic attack, and gently suggest how they can help you avoid another one."

She stared at him. Was this actually a possibility? It seemed too simple. "I'm not sure they would listen to me."

"That's why you give them a doctor's note." He smiled mischievously. "Just like high school phys ed."

Not quite. She'd loved high school phys ed, but she got his point. "I don't have time to get to a doctor's—" *Oh*. She gasped. "You think Hudson would do that for me?"

"I'm sure that he would. It's not like you're making something up. It's common sense. If someone has a panic attack, it has to be good medical advice to avoid the things that make them panic."

She sighed. "I guess it's worth a try."

He smiled and leaned in for a quick kiss. It was too quick. "Would you like a ride to Reno?"

She stared at him. Was he serious? She loved the idea of a road trip with this man, but that would have to wait. She sighed. "Actually, can you just give me a ride to the airport?"

He nodded, looking a little disappointed. "I can do that. Why don't you book your flight." He nodded toward the computer on the desk. "And I'll call Hudson and tell him to hurry up and get home."

Chapter 28

Dustin hung up the phone and looked at Mindy, who looked discouraged. "What is it?"

"It turns out there aren't a lot of flights between Rapid City and Reno. Like, there aren't any. None that would get me there by tomorrow night, anyway."

"Sorry. I didn't know that. I don't fly much." This was an understatement. He didn't fly at all.

"You don't have to be sorry. It's not your fault. But I don't know what to do now. I'm trying to think of another airport nearby that is bigger and might have better options."

Nearby was a relative term.

"How far are we from Denver?" she asked.

"About seven hours, but by the time we drive you to Denver, we've driven halfway to Nevada. Might as well keep going."

"Let me check." She turned back to the computer, and he thought about crossing his fingers that she wouldn't find something. He wanted her to get there in time, but he wanted to keep her right beside him till the last possible second. She gasped. "There is one!"

His heart sank.

"Gets me there about midnight. But oh my word it's a thousand dollars!" Her head fell on her chest. "Of course it is. It's a last-minute flight. I'm surprised it's not more. I'm an idiot. How did I think I was going to pay for this?"

"I'm happy to pay for it, but I'm sure if you called Vern"—*ugh*. He didn't like the way that man's name felt in his mouth.—"he would get the flight."

"Yeah, and then bill me for it," she said bitterly.

"Like I said, I'm happy to help."

She looked over her shoulder at him. "You're too good to me."

Someone has to be, he thought.

After a lingering look she returned her attention to the computer screen. She whimpered. "Never mind. You said it's seven hours to Denver?"

"Give or take."

"Then we can't get there in time." She leaned back and tipped her head back.

"Mindy." He spoke slowly, trying to make her get it. "I ... will ... drive ... you."

She spun the chair around and looked at him. "You really don't mind driving me to Reno?"

"Not only do I not mind, I want to do it."

"And we have time?"

"We'd better get going." He didn't know how long it would actually take.

"What about work? You said you don't have vacation for a while."

She wasn't wrong. "I could probably get tomorrow off. If we leave soon, I would only need to miss one day."

After a painfully long pause, she agreed.

"Good. Hudson will be here soon. You should go pack."

She snorted. "Pack my three outfits into my three plastic Walmart bags?"

Oh yeah. He'd forgotten about that. "I can probably find you a duffel bag around here somewhere."

She laughed. "You are a man with all the answers."

He was not, but he liked having her think that. "Speaking of being brilliant, you're probably going to want to bring a few costume pieces for disguise."

She cackled. "What?"

"I doubt you're going to be able to get from West Hope to Reno without using a public restroom, and unless you want to turn each of those into a meet and greet, maybe we should find you a scarf and some sunglasses. Or something."

"Does Chase have a scarf collection I could borrow from?"

"Ha-ha," he said sarcastically.

"Just kidding. I'll call Olivia." She got up, closed the gap between them, and kissed him lightly on the lips. "Are you sure about this?"

"Are you sure that you want to go to Reno?"

She nodded. "I think so."

"Then I'm sure that I want to take you." He was sure about something else too. Every second that he spent with Mindy Rose he fell deeper in love with her.

Chapter 29

Mindy couldn't believe that Dustin was going to drive her all the way to Reno. The destination was plugged into the GPS, and the GPS told them they only had eighteen hours to go. *Eighteen hours.* Had he known it would take that long when he'd volunteered? The man was a nut. If they were going to make it on time, they were going to have to drive straight through.

She stretched out her legs and tried to get comfortable. But then she glanced at Dustin's legs and felt guilty for feeling uncomfortable. He was one tall drink of water. Mindy was used to spending time on the road, but she usually did it with her own private bedroom, a television with a dozen streaming apps, and a kitchen of her own.

That bus had started to feel like a prison in recent months, but now she missed it. She would try not to take it for granted when she got back to it.

How cool would it be to take Dustin along on one of her tour legs? They would have too much fun on the bus. She would never get bored with him around. They could eat good food, watch bad movies, play cards, cuddle on the couch …"

"What are you thinking about?"

"Oh, uh … nothing."

"You were thinking about something. You were smiling."

Uh-oh. "I was?"

"You were. I figured it was something good."

Yeah, it sure had been. Her cheeks grew warm. Should she tell him that she'd been daydreaming about snuggling with him on her tour bus? *Nah.* Probably not. "I guess I'm just looking forward to getting back on the road."

"Oh good. So how does this costume thing work? Someone else picks out your clothes?"

"Yeah. They consider what's in style, what other people are wearing, what looks good on my body, what will appeal to my listeners, what matches my brand—"

"Good grief. I'm happy if something fits."

She giggled. "Yeah, most of the stuff they pick out *doesn't* fit me. Physically or metaphorically."

"So when you get there, you're going to be thrown right into rehearsal, right?"

"Probably."

"So if they agree to comply with your doctor's note, which I'm sure they will, will you have anything to wear? Are some of your options okay?"

"I doubt it. Usually they're all pretty bad."

"I was wondering if we should stop somewhere in Salt Lake City and get you an outfit."

She chuckled. "You want to go clothes shopping for me?"

"Well, no. I don't *want* to go, but I'm willing if that would be helpful to you."

She looked at the time. "Won't we be getting into Salt Lake in the middle of the night?"

"Oh yeah. Good point. I guess even a big city like that doesn't offer midnight clothes shopping."

She didn't want to tell him that Salt Lake wasn't a big city. "No, I don't think so. But it's a good idea. We could stop somewhere sooner."

"Uh, we're in Wyoming."

"So? People in Wyoming wear clothes, don't they?"

He chuckled. "Yeah, they kind of have to since it'll be twenty below here in a few months."

"So where do they buy those clothes?"

"I have no idea."

"What's the next town we hit?"

He glanced at his GPS. "Casper."

"Casper it is then. There must be clothes in Casper."

He snickered. "Oh boy. Let's get them to agree to your terms *before* they see the outfit you pick out in Casper."

"Okay, now I'm determined to prove you wrong. Can I borrow your phone?"

"Of course."

She typed "clothing Casper Wyoming" into her search bar. "Dude, there's a place called Cadillac Cowgirl!" She held her phone up and waggled it at him, though he couldn't see it from across the cab. "Cadillac Cowgirl! That *has* to be perfect. I'm going to look amazing."

"I stand corrected." He chuckled. "Maybe."

She clicked on their website and got even more excited. It had been a long time since she'd shopped for herself. But after a few minutes of virtually browsing the racks, she got car sick and had to look up. "How much farther till Casper?"

He laughed. "Quite a while, I'm afraid."

She sighed. "It sure is beautiful. I could live in Wyoming."

"There's no one here," he said matter-of-factly.

"Exactly."

He glanced at her. "You talk tough now, but you like people."

He was right, but she didn't want to admit it.

"Not much fun making music alone, no matter how good it is," he said.

"Fine. You win. If I lived in Wyoming, I would need to live in the city." She gazed out the window, watching the land fly by. "But it sure is gorgeous."

"Yes, yes it is."

They fell quiet for a moment, and she got lost in the views.

"What about Alabama?"

"Yeah. I love Alabama too, of course. It will always be home. And lately I've grown pretty fond of South Dakota. I guess I could live in lots of places."

"Keep popping out number one hits, and you'll be able to afford a home in every place you love."

She smiled. Wherever she lived, she hoped that Dustin Honeywood would be there.

Chapter 30

Dustin was struggling to think of something to say. They had music going, but he was too self-conscious to sing along. He couldn't imagine that she was self-conscious, but she wasn't singing either. "I'd offer to pass the time with some road games, but I can't think of any that would work in Wyoming."

"Road games? You mean like Yellow?"

"What's Yellow?"

"You get a point every time you are the first one to see a yellow car."

"So the first person to get one point wins?" He laughed at his own joke. She didn't join him. "We could play that you get a point if you're the first person to see a car of any color."

That made her laugh. "Okay. But that might get out of control when we hit Casper."

"Ah yes, the big city," he said. "And there's the game where we count cows, but again, when we finally see one, there's bound to be thousands of them. And there's the alphabet game where we find letters in order, but we've seen one billboard in the last hundred miles."

"Yeah. Maybe we don't play a road game. Maybe we … maybe we just converse. Like adults. Tell me all your hopes and dreams, Dustin Honeywood."

Oh boy. "Well, at the risk of disappointing you, I'm kind of a simple man."

"I don't believe that for a second."

"No really, I am. I've never wanted anything fancy. Though I do need to keep my mind occupied, or I chew shoes."

It took her a second to get the joke. "Oh, like a dog."

He laughed. "Yeah. Like a dog."

"Sorry. It's been a while since I had a dog."

"Well, we should remedy that soon."

She couldn't imagine having a dog with her life. The poor thing would be trapped on a bus. "So you like puzzles."

"I don't sit down and put together five-hundred-piece pictures of kittens, but yeah, I do get bored and fidgety if I don't have something to figure out. But other than that, I really am easy to please. I've never wanted much in life. Just to chill, have some fun, be happy."

"And were you envisioning a wife and family in that chill, happy mix?"

"Yeah. I was, as a matter of fact." This gave him an idea. "You know what would be way cooler than a road game?"

She didn't make a guess.

He glanced at her. "We could write a song that you'd want to sing."

She blew air through her lips. "They'd never let me sing it."

"Never say never, and even if they don't, it might be fun to try. But no pressure."

She stayed quiet for a long time. Assuming that she wasn't interested, he was disappointed. Not long after he'd recovered from that disappointment, she said, "Okay, let's give it a shot, but I probably won't be much help. Do you have any paper?"

"In the glove box. There's probably a pencil in there too if you root around a little."

She dug until she found what she needed. "Okay, what's our song about?"

"I don't know. What do you want to sing about?"

She chewed her lip. "I don't know."

"No, I mean, when you are up on stage singing 'Flirt till Flirty Fails,' what do you *wish* you were singing about?"

She let out a small gasp. "That's a good question. Um, I wish I was singing about real life. Like love and family, but also the hard stuff. Like songs about real people with real problems, but not necessarily depressing. I would want to sing about how life is hard, but it is also beautiful. Yeah! That's the crux of it. Life is hard, but it's also awesome. Because of things like love and family."

Every word she said made him more in love with her. "That sounds like a great song. So let's write it."

"Ugh. You make it sound so easy."

"No, it's not easy. It's a puzzle. That's why it's fun doing it."

He felt her eyes on him. "If you say so." Her pencil was poised over the paper. "Okay, how do we start?"

"We can start anyway you want. Sometimes I like to start with an image that puts me in the mood of the song. Sometimes I take the image out after, but it gets me going."

"Okay, what's the image?"

A dozen ideas sprang to mind, but he wanted her to feel like she contributed. "What do you think of when you think of real people with real problems and real love?"

Chapter 31

Real people with real problems and real love. That would be a long song title, but boy did Mindy like the sound of it. She thought they'd managed to define country music. Or at least what country music was supposed to be. She remembered the people broken down on the side of the road, the people who had essentially thrown the yogurt at the fan. "I think of a truck with its hood up and a woman stranded and maybe a little scared, and she's got kids with her, maybe a teenager, yeah, a teenager with a bad attitude. Yeah, that sounds pretty real."

He chuckled. "I knew it!"

"What?"

"I knew that you liked a puzzle too. That's going to be tricky to describe in a few lines, but you're right, it's a great image."

"Maybe we write a really long song."

He laughed again. "Free Bird."

Oh great, now she was going to have the "Free Bird" melody in her head. She stared at the paper. "You're going to have to give me some words. I told you I don't do this."

"You're doing it right now. You already came up with the idea and the image."

She knew what he was doing, and she loved him for it. "Okay, good. Then you come up with the first words."

"You see this woman and her kids in your head?"

"Sure."

"Great. Now you're pointing them out to me. What do you say?"

"Oh man. That stinks. They're stranded."

He laughed. "Poetic."

She groaned. "I *told* you. Don't make me do this and then make fun of me for being terrible at it. Maybe we should play Yellow."

"Still in Wyoming."

"Side of the road, nowhere Wyoming, stranded in the wind and sun." She gasped. Where had *that* come from? The words had just popped out of her.

"Brilliant. Write that down."

She did, as her tummy did tiny, excited back flips. "Okay, now what?"

"Now what rhymes with sun?"

"Fun?"

"Something that makes sense with the song."

"Oh. Yeah." She chuckled. "She fights the tears. What have I done?"

"Good. Write it."

She did. "Okay, I'm doing all the work here. You have to contribute, Mr. Songwriter."

"If I don't contribute, you don't have to pay me royalties."

She wanted to smack herself. It had never occurred to her that this could be a way that she could thank him for everything he'd done. Get him some song royalties! She had no idea how she could convince her people to let her cut this song, but now she was motivated to try. She looked down at the two lines. Well, if they actually ended up with a song.

"Teenaged daughter goes wild," he said. "No cell tower for miles and miles."

"That's clever, but I think I need to remove the mean teen from the mix."

He chuckled. "Oh really?"

"Yeah. More than half my fans are teenagers. I don't want to offend them."

"Oh, okay. Erase her then."

"I haven't written her down yet. How about this ... *Nowhere Wyoming, stranded in the wind and sun. Fighting tears, thinks what have I done? No cell towers, no white knight in sight. She's all alone as the sun sinks toward night.*"

"Whoa, this is getting a little depressing."

"Don't worry, I'm going to save her."

He laughed. "Good. Are you saving her soon, or are you going to make her wait till the bridge?"

"Zip it. I'm thinking."

He mimed zipping his lips shut.

"*She's real people in a real mess. With real fears she won't confess. With real wounds trying to heal* ..." And then, like this song had been orchestrated from the start, she heard Chase's voice. "*Good thing hope is real.*"

"Oh, whoa. That's good."

She hurried to write it down and then stared at it. "I don't know. It looks a little ..."

"We'll smooth it out when we add it to music. A good melody hides a lot of lyrical flaws."

She looked at him. "What are you, some kind of songwriting savant?"

He laughed. "Hardly. But I do like making up songs. Drove my mother nuts when we were little. I wrote the catchiest little number on branding."

Her heart jumped in excitement. "Sing it!" she cried.

He tightened his grip on the wheel. "I don't remember how it goes."

She stared at him. "Oh my word, you're lying to me right now. I thought you were a good man."

"Okay, fine. I might remember some of it, but I will not sing it in front of you no matter what."

Challenge accepted.

He glanced at the paper in her lap. "Now get back to work. You need a verse two."

"'Delta Dawn' got away with only one verse."

He gave her side-eye. "Why don't you write another just in case."

Chapter 32

They reached Casper in the nick of time, as Cadillac Cowgirl shut up shop at five o'clock. The only person working the closing shift was a young woman who recognized Mindy right away. But Dustin had to give her credit for not freaking out and fangirling.

Her eyes got wide, she looked at Mindy, looked long at Dustin, and then looked back at Mindy and breathed, "It's you." But then she came to her senses. "Please let me know if you need any help."

"Actually, I do. What's your name?"

The woman looked startled to be asked. "Natalie."

"Great. Hi, Natalie. I need an outfit. A little bit dressy but not formal or anything. Colorful but not brazen. Cute but not childish. Fun but not trampy."

Somehow, Natalie took this all in. "Okay, let me get you some options. She buzzed around her store, plucking things off the racks. As she grabbed the third shirt, Mindy said, "Hang on. Can I see that?"

The woman held it up.

"Yeah. If it fits, that's the one. Now I need some high waisted jeans. And if they've got holes in them, all the better."

She started to dart off and then hesitated. Her eyes traveled up and down Mindy's body. "How about a jean skirt? I have a really good one."

Dustin almost laughed. Was this woman giving Mindy Rose fashion advice?

Natalie must have sensed his silent criticism because she hurriedly added, "I don't work on commission or anything. It's a good skirt."

Mindy nodded. "Okay, let's try it."

Natalie scurried off, fully invested in this mission. She came back with a denim skirt with small holes in it. Mindy snatched it out of her hand and took it into the dressing room along with the magical shirt. She came out seconds later and did a three-sixty twirl for them to see.

Natalie clapped. "Gorgeous! Now what about your shoes?"

Mindy looked down at her worn cowboy boots. "I'm wearing these."

Natalie grimaced. "Are you sure?"

Mindy smiled brightly. "I'm sure."

"Okay, well, if you don't mind me saying, you're looking a little ..." She held her hand out toward Misty and waved it around like she was trying to move things with her mind. She sighed. "Dull."

"Yeah," Mindy said. "That's kind of what I was going for."

Natalie nodded, her expression grave. "I get it. You don't want to look ostentatious."

Ostentatious? Dustin wasn't sure he had a firm grasp on what that meant.

"Exactly," Mindy said.

Natalie put her hands on her hips. "We've either got to upgrade the shirt or the boots. You choose."

This time Dustin did laugh. "I think she's okay. We've got to get going."

But Mindy was turning toward the mirror. "No, she's right. The stage lights are going to wash these colors out."

Natalie squealed. "You're wearing this on stage?"

Without turning around, Mindy looked at her in the mirror and nodded.

"The boots! The boots!" Natalie cried and then took off running.

She came back with tall, bright red cowboy boots.

To Dustin's dismay, Mindy's eyes lit up. "We've got to get goin', darlin'." They still had a lot of road ahead of them.

Mindy shook her head at Natalie, completely ignoring him. "Meet me in the middle. Those are too bright."

Natalie kept her disagreement silent and went to find more boots. Dustin looked at the clock.

Mindy tried on every pair of boots in the store. None of them were right. "I'm telling you," Natalie said. "The red ones."

"Okay, fine. The red ones."

Natalie narrowed her eyes. "Don't you dare buy them and then wear the old ones on stage."

Mindy laughed. "I won't. I promise."

Natalie looked at Dustin. "You hold her to that."

Yeah, like he was going to have any say in her foot wardrobe. He was going to be halfway back to Casper by the time she took the stage.

Finally, they checked out, and Mindy promised to pay him back every penny. "I'm not worried about it," he said until he saw the price of those boots. But then he convinced himself it was still okay.

Natalie handed Mindy a business card. "You give me a ring if you need anything. I can also find stuff and order it if that's helpful."

Mindy looked thoughtful. "It actually will be helpful. Thank you, Natalie. I mean it." She took the bag.

"You're welcome, and I mean it. It's good to see that you're okay."

Chapter 33

Mindy pulled Olivia's hat on tight and donned her sunglasses, stepped out of Cadillac Cowgirl, and saw the Mexican restaurant directly across the street. Her stomach roared to life. This was a good thing; she hadn't felt this hungry in a long time. "Let's grab a burrito."

"Mindy, we really have to get going. We've got a long way to—"

She grabbed his hand and tugged. "Come on, we'll get it to go."

Dustin let her tug him into the restaurant. "You know, driving in an unfamiliar city while munching on enchiladas probably isn't the best combination."

"You're right. Let's eat here." She wasn't stalling, exactly, but neither was she in a hurry for this extended date to end. She looked at the menu, and her stomach sank. "Oh my word, I did it again."

He looked at her. "What's that?"

"I keep forgetting that I don't have any money."

"You do have money. You just don't have any on you. And I'm not worried about it."

She admired him. He sure was one handsome white knight. "Thank you. I am turning into one expensive project."

He laughed. "You're not a project. Now, that song we penned? *That* was a project. I'm still not sure we've got it right."

"We do," she assured him. "I've never been so proud of anything." She couldn't wait to sing it for the label. She was certain it was good enough to cut. "It's going to make you rich and famous."

He belted out a laugh. "I doubt that. Hey, speaking of rich and famous, there's another musician from West Hope, you know."

"There is?" Instantly she felt guilty for sounding so surprised. "Who?"

"Shane Bannon?"

"Oh yeah!" She didn't know him personally, but she knew who he was. "Are you friends with him?"

"Not really. We've got a nod-at-each-other-in-the-grocery-store re-lationship, but that's it."

She laughed. She knew what he meant. "Shane Bannon. Wow. I haven't heard that name in a while."

"Yeah, I think he might be done with the Nashville scene. He moved home to be with his wife and daughter."

She sighed wistfully. "Can't blame him there."

He reached for her hand. "Your situation is a little different. You've got time for both career and family."

She smiled. "Thanks. I sure hope so."

They ordered their food and then found a table. The place was crazy busy, and it seemed they didn't have enough staff to keep up. "Wow," Dustin said. "Too bad we didn't live closer. Olivia could work here."

"Is she looking for a restaurant job?"

"Not really. Wyatt is helping her get a catering business going."

"Oh, yeah, that makes sense. Is she going to cater the ranch's events?"

"I think that's part of the plan, yeah. If they ever get any events scheduled." He eyed her. "Speaking of which, you do know that those boots you just bought are the same color as that awful Cadillac."

She gasped. "No, they're not!"

"Yes, they *are*."

He was wrong. He was just messing with her. "Well, I can't take them back. I'm sure Natalie has closed up shop by now."

"Natalie is probably calling everyone she knows and telling them what happened."

"Oh no." Her mind started spinning. "I didn't think of that." She looked out the window.

"What? Didn't think of what?"

"If she tells people, they might come here. I should have let you leave town."

"Don't worry about it. No one paid us any mind crossing the street, and no one here seems to recognize you. If she tells them, they'll probably assume that you're long gone."

She nodded. "Okay. Thank goodness for Olivia's hat."

"Hey!" Dustin moved his arms off the table. "Here comes our food!"

It was worth the wait. "Wow, this is delicious. It tastes so authentic."

"It probably is." He downed half of his water.

She giggled. "A little spicy?"

He filled his fork again. "Yeah, but it's worth it."

She heard something at the window and looked up to see a gaggle of teenage girls gawking through it excitedly.

Dustin sighed. "I don't think they're looking at the tacos."

Chapter 34

B y the time they left Casper, it was nine o'clock. "It's late," Mindy said, "I should call my mom. Can I use your phone for a sec, or do you need the GPS?"

"Just let me get on the right road, and then it's the same road for a long time." He chuckled. "It's the only road, I think." He didn't think he would get lost in Casper, but the sun had gone down, which made him feel like he was pressed for time. He didn't want to have to take any accidental detours.

He got them on the right road without any rerouting. "Okay, I think I'm good. Go ahead."

He could hear the affection in Mindy's voice. It was obvious that her mom was easily confused, but Mindy was able to make her understand that she was headed back to work. Everything was okay, and she would see her soon.

"How soon is soon?" he asked when she hung up. "I mean, how often do you get to see her?"

"Whenever we're in the south, we swing through and stop. And if I have a day off somewhere, especially if I have two, I try to fly home and see her for a while. It's getting harder because flying commercial can be pretty dramatic these days. I used to be able to get away with it if I wore sunglasses, but not so much anymore."

"You're a pretty big deal."

"Yeah." She sighed. "Can't believe I thought you didn't recognize me."

"To be fair, Hudson and Chase really didn't recognize you. And Olivia didn't at first."

"I think Chase might have. He just didn't want to deal with it."

Dustin laughed. "Yeah. Maybe." They might never know. Chase was good at keeping secrets.

They fell silent as they drove, and soon Dustin felt an eerie isolation. They hadn't seen another vehicle in a really long time, and his phone showed absolutely no signal.

"Where on earth are we?" Mindy might have been feeling it too.

"Wyoming." He was trying to be funny, trying not to let his nervousness show. He was a little weirded out that he even *was* nervous. He was from South Dakota. He had driven through desolation before, but this—this was something a little different, a bit more ... severe.

"Can you feel that wind?" she asked.

He sure could. "Yeah, but it's no big deal." He wasn't sure if he sounded nonchalant, but he was really trying. "This is Wyoming. It's always windy."

"But why can't I see anything? I mean, it feels like we're driving through the sky. I wish the moon was out."

So did he. It did feel like they were hurtling through outer space, all alone. What he would give for an eighteen-wheeler to follow for a while. "I believe this is what they call the high desert plains."

"High desert," she mused. "No wonder my ears are going nuts."

"Yeah, I saw an elevation sign a while back. It said seven thousand feet."

"I saw that too. And it feels like we've gone higher since then."

"Well, I think we are driving over the continental divide, so we're pretty high."

She groaned. "And to think that I was relieved we didn't have to go through the Rockies."

"You must go through the Rockies pretty often."

"Not really. We try to go around them."

He chuckled. "Yeah. I guess your bus probably doesn't love hairpin turns."

"No hairpin turns here. No turns at all." She chuckled, but he could feel her unease.

"Hey, I know it's unsettling, but there's really nothing to worry about."

"No? What if you hit a buffalo, and then we get out of the truck and get blown away, and no one ever finds us? They'll think I've run off again."

He couldn't tell if she was exaggerating or if she was really freaking out. "Mindy, if we hit a buffalo, stay in the truck."

She laughed. "Okay."

"Don't worry. Whatever comes our way, I will protect you." Or die trying. "Hey look, a sign! Pathfinder National Wildlife Refuge."

She groaned. "Oh my word, the buffalo actually own this land!"

He laughed pretty hard at this, which made him feel lighter. A gust of wind blew his truck off course, but he easily brought it back. "Don't worry. We're almost through to the next town."

"What's the next town?"

He had no idea. He also wasn't sure they were anywhere near it, but it had sounded good. "I can't think of the name." He could feel her nervousness, and it was contagious. He was going to feel really stupid and be really mad at himself if he got them both killed out here in the middle of nowhere. At least it was June—they probably wouldn't freeze to death. "Why don't you put on some music?"

"No, thank you."

He laughed at her forthrightness.

Another sign came into view. "Hey, we're on the Oregon Trail!" He didn't have to fake excitement about this. He found it pretty cool. Those people had pulled wagons over the continental divide? Although now that he thought about it, of course they did. How else would they have gotten to the other side?

She let out a strangled cry.

"What, you don't like history?"

"No, I do." She said this through clenched teeth.

"Well, that wasn't very convincing. Those people did just fine in their wagons. I think we'll be okay in this truck."

"Did just fine?" she screeched. "They all died of dysentery!"

He laughed again, so hard that he felt guilty. Here she was genuinely scared, and he couldn't stop laughing, but eventually she joined him, and though they kept talking all the way back to civilization, she never sounded scared again.

Chapter 35

When they hit the Nevada state line, Dustin pulled into a rest area and looked at her. "I need a break."

"I would imagine. Do you want me to drive for a while?"

He hesitated.

"Do you not trust me?"

"No, it's not that. But you've got to be just as tired as I am."

"Yes, but my stress is keeping me awake."

He chuckled.

"If you don't want me to, or if you're not going to be able to relax if I do, no worries. But I can drive if you want me to."

He nodded. "Okay. But please don't crash because that will probably wake me up."

She laughed as she got out of the truck. "I'm going to go use the facilities. I'll be right back." She pulled her hat down and her collar up as she hurried across the lot. She kept her head down, and no one inside noticed her. It probably helped that it was the wee hours of the morning, and everyone was half asleep. By the time she got back to the truck, Dustin was already snoring, his arms folded across his chest, his head lolling against the window, and his hat pulled down over his eyes.

For a second she panicked that she didn't know how to get where she was going, but then she remembered that from here on out, it was all I-80 all the time. "Just stay on eighty," she whispered to herself.

Mountains rose to her right and in the distance in front of her. The first hints of a new day bathed the landscape in a thousand shades of orange. As the light grew stronger, her fatigue came on rapidly. She'd been wide awake all night but now that the sun was coming up, her circadian clock was lurching like it was learning to drive a stick for the first time.

She didn't think she was going to fall asleep, but wow, was she tired.

She wanted to pull over for a coffee or a coke or some candy, but she'd only just started driving, and she didn't want to wake Dustin up. He'd earned this nap.

In so many different ways.

How many times had her bus drivers driven through the night for her? She'd never known how brutal this time of day was for someone who'd been up all night. She was never going to take them for granted again. In fact, maybe she could see about getting them a pay raise. She wasn't really in charge of stuff like that, but maybe that could change. She sneaked a peek at Dustin; she had a feeling lots of things in her life would be changing in the near future.

At least now there were other vehicles on the road. Mostly eighteen wheelers, but still, they were no longer the lone pickup flying through the frontier. She found that comforting.

She straightened in her seat and tightened her grip on the wheel. She wished she could turn the music up, but that would wake Dustin. Actually, she wished she could *change* the music up. She was sick to death of his playlist. But she didn't want to fiddle with his phone while she was driving.

So she listened to "Straight Tequila Night" for the tenth time, and she kept heading west as the sun kept adding more and more colors to the earth's palette. Her eyes burned, and her eyelids felt heavy, but the raw beauty was not lost on her. She needed to pay more attention to the countryside while she was crisscrossing it. She was missing so much.

Maybe she and Dustin could write a song that captured just how breathtakingly beautiful America was. The spirit of it. The variety of it. The majesty of it. No wonder the early settlers and explorers were so smitten. So was she right now.

Her eyelids started to get a little too hot and too heavy, so she slapped her face, not hard enough to truly hurt, just hard enough to sting a little—it worked. It perked her right up, but Dustin also stirred, so she didn't try that again. Apparently even while unconscious Dustin was intent on protecting her, even from herself.

When Dustin opened his eyes just east of Winnemucca, she was both disappointed and relieved.

"Please stop at the next opportunity," he said. "I need some coffee."

She glanced at the clock. "You can go back to sleep. You didn't sleep very long."

"Oh no," he said quickly. "I feel great. Thanks for letting me get some rest."

As if he was the one who needed to be thanking her.

He looked at her. "How are you holding up?"

"Pretty tired," she admitted.

"Yeah, I'll bet. Where are we?"

"Winnemucca."

"Yeah, that means nothing to me." He chuckled as she moved over to the exit lane and slowed down.

"I don't know much about it either. I've just been seeing the signs."

"Nevada is a big state."

She laughed. "Yes, yes it is. America's a big country."

"Yeah," he said, and he sounded sad.

Chapter 36

"Whoa. This place is huge." Dustin drove past the Reno events center, looking for a parking lot. He would die of nerves if he had to get on a stage in a place this big. "How many people fit in a place like this?"

"This one's not even that big. Seven thousand seats, and we sold out."

"That's big."

"Oh yeah," she said quickly. "It is. I just meant that I've played bigger."

He couldn't wrap his brain around it. "Must be so trippy hearing seven thousand voices singing your lyrics."

"They're not my lyrics, but yes, I get your point, and I imagine it would be way more powerful if I'd written them. I would think that they would be here by now. Would you mind driving around? Maybe we'll see my bus."

His stomach twisted into a knot. The woman he'd been hanging around with for the past few days, the relatively normal, albeit gorgeous, woman—she had a *bus*. A bus of her own. That felt so surreal. Maybe he hadn't been framing all of this the right way. He'd been thinking of her as an equal. Talented and successful, sure, but still just a woman like any other woman. But maybe he'd been wrong. Because right now he felt like he was driving around with a woman from a different universe.

"There." She pointed.

And now he was staring at a giant shiny tour bus. If it weren't for the fact that Mindy's face was emblazoned on the side, he might have mistaken it for a spaceship.

He looked at that face, so different from the one he felt like he knew. His stomach sank as he realized he did *not* know the woman painted on that bus. Not even close.

"Are you okay?" Her fingers rested expectantly on the door handle.

He'd stopped the truck and then stared stupidly up at the bus. He put his truck in park and turned off the engine. "Yeah, sorry. Was just thinking that your bus costs more than my house."

"Maybe, but I don't have a house so I'm not really up on house prices." She laughed lightly, but her laugh quickly faded as she sensed he wasn't okay. "Are you still going to go in with me?"

Did she really need him to? "If you want me to." He hoped she didn't. He was out of his element, and he didn't like the feeling.

"If you don't mind." She studied him. "I feel stronger when you're around."

It was a nice compliment, but he had trouble believing it. "Okay." He got out of the truck, hating how unsure of himself he suddenly felt. He took a deep breath and gave himself a silent pep talk. *You are still you, and these people are just people. Just be who you are.*

"Do you want a tour?"

It took him a second to realize that she was talking about the bus. "Oh! Sure."

"Great." She sounded excited and proud, which was cute. He followed her to the door, which opened when she got there.

"Well it's about time," a man said, his smile letting them know that he wasn't actually scolding her.

She flung her arms around him. "Thanks, Mike. It's good to see you too."

"You had us worried, kiddo. Good to see you're okay."

"I'm sorry. I didn't mean to scare anyone."

"You're forgiven. I put your phone in your purse." He nodded toward the closet.

"Oh, thank you so much! If I'd known I was going to freak out and run off stage, I would have brought my phone with me."

He chuckled.

"Do you know where Vern is?"

Mike nodded. "I can take you to him."

"Okay, just a sec. This is my awesome friend Dustin, and I want to show him the bus."

Mike offered a handshake. "So we have you to thank for whisking her away?"

Dustin opened his mouth to protest, but Mindy did it for him. "No, none of this is his fault. In fact, he's the one who convinced me to come back."

Mike's eyebrows went up as he pumped Dustin's hand up and down enthusiastically. "Ah, you're a hero then!"

The praise embarrassed Dustin, but he tried not to show it. He didn't feel like much of a hero right now.

"So this is the living room." Mindy swept her arm across the small space.

"Looks comfy."

"It is. It's nice to be able to stretch out your legs when you're on the road."

Sorry that you were cramped while I drove all night, he thought bitterly.

"And this is the kitchen, though we don't use it much." She rubbed her stomach. "Way too much takeout." She took a few steps and flung open a door. "And this is my closet!" She pretended to retch. "Hope its contents improve soon." She spun down the narrow hallway, pointing. "This is the bathroom." She flung open a door. "And this is my teeny tiny bedroom!" She plopped down on the end of a bed that almost stretched from wall to wall. She patted the bed beside her.

Uncomfortably, he sat.

"I spend way too much time in here," she muttered as if this was some deep dark confession. She looked at the TV on the wall. "And I watch way too much TV." She smiled at him. "I used to try to read, but I get car sick. So! Want to join me some time?"

What? Was she serious?

"I mean, when you can get some vacation? I'd love to take you on the road with me." She elbowed him playfully.

He couldn't even imagine that. Part of him got excited at the thought. Part of him warned the first part not to get excited. This was all a mirage, and soon his vision would clear.

She popped up, reached down, took his hand, and pulled him to his feet. "Come on, let's go face the music. Literally."

Chapter 37

M indy wondered if she was going to be sick. She had a pretty good relationship with Vern, but she had really burned him with all this, and she was scared to deal with that fallout. But she kept her chin up as she and Dustin followed Mike down the dark back hallways of the event center.

Her fears were not alleviated at the sight of his face. "You're late."

"I am?" She was pretty sure they had time to spare.

"Yeah. Several days late." Vern looked at Dustin. "Can I help you?"

Though her sick feeling was as strong as ever, something in her strengthened at the attack on Dustin. "No. He doesn't need your help. And he's the reason I'm here, so how about you be civil?"

Vern's eyes widened. She had never talked back to him. Ever. She'd always felt beholden to him. She owed her career to him.

She felt less beholden now.

A smattering of people bustled about behind him, pretending to mind their own business. She straightened her spine and rolled her shoulders back. "Is there somewhere we could talk privately? It won't take long."

Vern glanced at Dustin and then returned his eyes to her before nodding. If she didn't know better, she would think he almost looked nervous. He led them through a door and into an overly air-conditioned conference room. It took him a minute to find the light switch, but once he did, he turned to face her and crossed his arms in front of his body.

"I've seen a doctor," she began, just like she'd silently rehearsed as she'd traveled halfway across the country. "And he thinks that what I experienced in Deadwood was a panic attack."

The words did not surprise him.

She inhaled deeply. "The good news is, he also thinks it will be really easy for me to avoid having another one."

Vern cocked one eyebrow. "Is that right?" He knew what was coming.

"That's right. He thinks there were a few factors that caused the attack and that if I avoid those factors, I'll be okay."

"And did he prescribe you any medication?"

"He doesn't think we're there yet." She assumed this part. Hudson had not offered a prescription. "Avoiding the things that make me panic seems a simpler solution—"

"Not if the things that make you panic are *part of your job.*"

"They are not," she said with a confidence she didn't necessarily feel.

He grimaced. "So what are you asking to avoid?"

Okay, enough with the attitude. Had Vern always been like this? "I'm not *asking* anything. I'm *telling* you that I will no longer be recording songs that make me morally uncomfortable, and I'm *telling* you that I will be making wardrobe decisions from now on." She searched his impassive face for some clue. He didn't seem horrified. He almost looked … *relieved?* Was that possible? What had he expected her to demand?

But he wasn't agreeing to her conditions either. He was only staring back at her, his jaw tight. "You can have some input as to wardrobe, but you're not wearing whatever you want. That's why we have a stylist. She knows what she's doing."

"I'm not going to wear anything that makes me uncomfortable, Vern." She shook her head. "Not anymore."

He threw up his hands. "Fine. So what are you wearing tonight then?"

She smiled broadly and held her arms out. "Don't I look amazing? I hired a *stylist* in Casper, Wyoming."

He sneered. "Rebecca might quit."

"Fine, then. I'll call my backup. She's in Casper, Wyoming."

Beside her Dustin choked on a laugh.

"You're not changing the set list."

"Of course not." Was he even listening? "I won't stop singing the songs I've already cut because the fans love those songs. But I'm not cutting any more songs about getting drunk and sleeping around."

He took a step back, let out a weird grunting sound, and mumbled, "I should've known you were too much of a prude for this business." He gave Dustin a dirty look and then started to walk away. "Get to the stage. Everyone's waiting for you."

She waited till he was out of sight before flinging her arms around Dustin. She gave him a tight squeeze and then pulled back so she could gaze at his face, but she kept her hands locked around his neck. "Did you hear that? I'm a prude!"

He smiled and laid his hands lightly on her waist. "Doesn't prudent mean that you make good decisions for your future? I'd take it as a compliment."

She couldn't stop smiling. "I don't think that's the way he meant it, but thank you." Her joy started to dissipate, and she wasn't sure why. Was Dustin sad? "We did it," she said softly.

"*You* did it." His voice was tender, vulnerable. She hadn't heard him speak like that before.

"But I couldn't have done it without you."

"Well, good thing you picked the right truck to hide out in then."

There, that was more like the playful Dustin she knew. She kissed him lightly on the lips. "Right. Good thing I didn't pick the sewer truck."

He barely smiled.

"Really? I thought that would get a bigger laugh." She sighed. "I wish you could stay for the show."

He started pulling away. "I have to get back, but I'll take a rain check?"

She nodded. "Deal." A lump formed in her throat. She didn't want to let go of him. "I don't know how to thank you."

"You thank me by being happy." Why was he sounding like this was a forever-goodbye?

"I am happy, especially when I'm with you. So let me iron out the kinks, and then I'll try to get a few days off to come see you?"

He nodded, but she could tell that he didn't believe her. What was going on with him?

"Hey." She shook him a little. "I mean it. I'm not letting you get away."

A small grin formed on his lips. "Okay."

"Okay." She kissed him again and then stepped back, grabbing one of his hands. She really didn't want to let go of him, and him acting like this was the end of something was scaring her. "Are we okay?"

His regretful expression transformed into a goofy grin. "Of course we're okay!"

She studied him. He was being fake right now. He was acting like he was on stage. "So I'll call you after the show?"

He nodded. "Okay." He pulled his hand away and backed toward the door. "It's been awesome knowing you, Mindy. You go knock 'em dead." He winked, and then he turned and swiftly walked away.

She watched the door close behind him and started to freak out. Was she making a mistake? She loved her career, but she loved him too. But couldn't she have both? Hadn't they agreed to that? No, not really. She'd made some assumptions, but he'd never really promised anything.

Her chest hurt, and her legs itched to run after him. But if she did that again, her career really might be over. And her mother needed her.

She shook her head. *Stop being paranoid. You can call him after the show.* Yes, she would do that, and then she would call him every single day after that, and she would get back to West Hope as soon as she could, and this time she would make him promise.

Promise to be hers.

Chapter 38

Dustin pointed his truck northeast and headed in the opposite direction from where his heart was tugging him.

What had he been thinking? No, that was a stupid question. He knew what he'd been thinking. He'd found a beautiful woman in the back of his truck, a woman in need, a witty, charming, smart woman in need—and he'd fallen for her. He'd either allowed himself to pretend that she wasn't a rich superstar, or he'd really been so dumb as to not realize it.

He sighed. He knew one thing for sure: this hurt more than he thought it would.

He rubbed his eyes. He was so tired. His little Nevada nap hadn't done much to stave off the exhaustion of driving all night. He had planned to drive until dark. He figured that would put him near Salt Lake City, where he would easily be able to find a hotel. This had been his plan even before he had made himself nervous in the desolate Wyoming wilderness. But now, knowing how much he'd enjoyed that stretch of road, his plan seemed even better. The route wouldn't be nearly as disconcerting in daylight; he also thought maybe the daylight would show him that he'd had no reason to be nervous in the first place.

But he didn't think he would make it to Salt Lake City.

He didn't want to stop yet, though, or he'd have a miserably long drive the next day. It had been fun driving nonstop with Mindy riding shotgun. It wasn't so fun now. He glanced at her empty side of the truck, and it felt like someone was ripping a chunk out of his chest. How had he been so stupid to let himself get so attached?

It was Mindy Rose, for crying out loud. You've seen her on award shows. You've heard her on the radio. She's a superstar. She's not just some girl.

He turned the music up and kept driving. He would push as far as he could and try to get as close to Salt Lake City and home as he could.

One mile at a time, he told himself. *You're going to recover from this.* He knew this was true. He knew this wouldn't hurt forever. But man did it smart right now.

He forced himself to sing along with "Seminole Wind," and he kept driving.

Chapter 39

M indy could hear them screaming her name, and her stomach filled with nerves. She didn't really get stage fright anymore, but this was different. She climbed up onto the hydraulic lift and nodded to her stagehand that she was ready. She adjusted her earpiece for the seventieth time as the lift started raising her. *Help me, God. Help me give them a good show.*

The manufactured smoke whirled around her head, and she lifted the microphone to her mouth and gave them the first few lines of her opening song before they'd seen her. Their screaming grew louder—because they'd heard her voice, but also because she was growing closer. Then she was above the stage level, and she could see the faces in the front row. She gave them a big smile as she belted out the lyrics they loved. The lift kept going, and soon she was up in the air looking down on them. The spotlight blinded her, and she closed her eyes and focused on her voice, hitting the notes, sounding strong, putting the emotion into the words.

This is pretty fun, she thought. She hadn't realized how much she'd missed this. It was so incredible that she got to do this, that people *paid her* to do this. She should be paying them, she thought. Her shows always went by in such a blur. Her adrenaline carried her, she gave it her all, and then after the show, she could barely remember having been on stage. But this time she tried to capture the feeling. She wanted to remember how this felt. She looked out at the fans and focused on individual faces. She wanted to remember them. The two teen girls jumping up and down to the right. The woman in the cowboy hat with tears streaming down her face. The man beside her who looked like he'd rather be watching football. She winked at him, and he gave her a crooked grin that reminded her of Chase Honeywood.

Her heart lurched. The Honeywoods. She missed them already.

She shook that thought out of her head and focused on what she was doing. She wanted to remember every second of this.

When the Reno show was over, Mindy couldn't remember much. More than usual, but still—not much. She vowed to ask more seasoned performers for tips and tricks. There had to be a way to slow down the experience in her head and preserve some of those moments. She didn't want to look back on these nights and not be able to recall anything. She felt so high when she was out there on stage. She wanted to be able to recall that feeling in the future.

Usually the first thing she did after a show was rip off her clothes and get into her pajamas, and she started to do just that as soon as she was safely aboard her bus, but then she realized that she wasn't uncomfortable. She looked down at the Casper outfit that had served her so well and smiled. She didn't need to escape from this skirt and blouse.

She changed slowly, without the normal horror and rage, and then she crawled onto the bed. She was exhausted. And then she remembered that her phone was still in the closet. She dragged herself up, but as soon as she had the phone in her hand, she collapsed again. Of course it was dead. She plugged it in and lay it beside her. Just as soon as it had enough charge to turn on, she would call Dustin. She couldn't wait.

The squeaking of the bus's brakes woke Mindy up. *Oh no!* She grabbed her phone, hoping she hadn't slept for long.

It was quarter past three in the morning. She groaned.

Now what? She couldn't call him at three in the morning. Granted, he might be awake and driving, but she didn't know that, and if he had pulled over to get some sleep, she didn't want to wake him up. Should she text him? No, the notification might wake him up.

Stop panicking. Just call in the morning. Okay. She would call around seven and apologize profusely. He would understand. He was a reasonable man. He wasn't a jerk.

It wasn't all going to fall apart just because she was late with one phone call. She knew this was true. So why was there this foreboding in her gut?

Chapter 40

The morning sun shone through the thin motel curtains, warming Dustin's face. He rubbed his eyes and sat up. He was still tired, but he was glad he'd pushed himself. He hadn't made it to Salt Lake City, but he'd made it to Utah. He stood up and stretched. Only twelve hours to go.

If everything went well, he could do all of Wyoming in daylight.

He picked up his phone to check the time. Oh wow, he'd slept late. He had to get going then. He had two missed calls: one from Hudson and one from an out-of-state number he didn't recognize. He also had a text.

"Hey, it's Mindy. So sorry, my phone was dead last night, and I accidentally fell asleep waiting for it to charge. But it's charged now, so call me when you can! I miss you." Despite himself and his efforts at masculinity, he couldn't help but smile at the emoji blowing a heart kiss that she'd added at the end.

He opened the app to text back and then froze. What was he going to say? "No worries," he typed. "I miss you too." No, that was too needy. He erased it and stared at the phone. Ugh. He needed coffee. He dropped the phone on the bed. He would text her when he got some coffee.

Fifteen minutes later Dustin was on the road in search of caffeine. He found it at a Sinclair gas station five minutes later. He added more cream than necessary and then drank half of it on the way back to his truck.

He slammed the door behind him, started the truck to get the AC blowing, and then eyed the phone. Why was he so nervous? He took a deep breath, hit the call button, and put it on speaker. Then he started driving as it rang.

And rang and rang.

She wasn't going to answer. What could she be doing at nine in the morning? Wasn't she just curled up in her expensive house-on-wheels watching television? Her recorded voice told him to leave a message, but his tongue was tied in knots. He hit the button on the steering wheel to hang up.

He would text her next time he stopped.

He called Burke instead.

Burke answered.

"Hey, where are you?" Dustin asked.

"Where am I? I'm in West Hope. Where are *you*? Seth told me that you're driving to Nevada to hand deliver a country music star?" He laughed. "Now I know that can't be true."

Burke was right. It didn't sound true. "Yeah. I already dropped her off. I'm headed home now. You could have warned me about Wyoming." Dustin knew that Burke had driven every road in Wyoming. It was sort of his shtick. There had been talk of him moving to Wyoming, but his wife didn't want to. Ava said that if he was always going to be at the rodeo, she wanted to be near her family, not all alone in some weird Wyoming town.

Burke laughed. "Which Wyoming warning was I supposed to give? It's June. I'm pretty sure there's no chain law in effect right now."

"Maybe not, but Route 220 tried to kill me."

The familiar joviality of Burke's deep laugh brought Dustin immense comfort. "Well, why did you take the Oregon Trail?"

"Because the GPS told me too."

"Come on, man. Following the GPS in Wyoming is asking for trouble."

"Well, you weren't here to help me with your brain maps."

"I would have gone. No one invited me."

"Weren't you in Missouri?"

He chuckled. "Yeah, I guess I was."

"How'd that go?" Dustin knew it hadn't gone great, or he would have heard about it.

"Still in one piece. For real, you should go to Wyoming with me sometime, and I'll show you some roads that are actually hairy."

Dustin rolled his eyes. "Tempting offer, but I'm probably not going to use my few vacation days to drive around Wyoming with you." He'd rather use them to see Mindy—if she still remembered who he was by then.

"Fine. Your loss."

Dustin laughed. "Anyway, glad you made it home safely. I'm on my way. I don't know how you're on the road so much. I am ready to get out of this truck."

"Yeah. I don't know. I just like driving around. Call me when you get here. Me and Ava will bring takeout, and you can tell us all about your new sweetheart."

"Deal. I'll gladly eat your food, but I don't think Mindy Rose is my sweetheart."

Chapter 41

Three times Mindy had picked up the phone to call Dustin, and three times she'd been interrupted. And the one time he'd called her, she'd been in the shower. When they finally pulled into Portland, she was excited to get off the bus and find a quiet spot to call him from, but then Vern reminded her that she had a radio interview to get to.

She tried to hide her disappointment. She loved local radio dearly and didn't want anyone to think otherwise just because she was mad about her lack of free time.

The bus dropped her and three of her people off in front of the station, and though they tried to usher her inside immediately, a woman did recognize her and stop her for a picture. This of course made others stop, and soon a line had formed. She didn't mind and made Vern be the bad guy who had to end the session to get her into the building on time.

The host was a sharply dressed woman in her forties who immediately gave Mindy a bad feeling. Country music people were usually so friendly that she tried to convince herself that she was wrong about this one—but the feeling wouldn't go away. One thing became increasingly clear: Christy was one confident woman. A faded poster on the wall behind Christy's chair showed a younger Christy with big hair on a fairgrounds stage. Mindy smiled and pretended to be interested. "What a great photo!" It wasn't. It was blurry. "Where was that?"

"That's my band," Christy said, not telling her where it was taken.

Fair enough. *Just get this over with.* Mindy sat and put her headphones on.

Christy introduced her to the listeners and then said, "Now, let's get down to business, shall we?"

Mindy smiled, mostly because she knew the listeners would be able to hear the smile in her tone. "Sure."

"Congratulations are in order. 'Flirt Till Flirty Fails' climbed all the way to number two!"

Mindy wasn't fooled. This was a jab. Christy was calling attention to the fact that the song had *only* hit number two. It was Mindy's first single in a while that hadn't gone to number one. Mindy hadn't been surprised. It was a terrible song with an embarrassing video. "Thank you. I was quite pleased that it made it that far."

Christy narrowed her beady little eyes. It was clear how the media professional hadn't ended up on television. "That's great. But what the listeners really want to know is, what happened in Deadwood?"

Mindy was ready for this. She'd spoken with her publicist, who had thrown out a dozen ridiculous spins. Mindy had listened politely and then said, "I'm going to tell the truth." The publicist hadn't liked this, of course, and Mindy had appeased her by promising to leave out some of the details.

Mindy hadn't really wanted to tell her fans that she'd hidden in a water truck wearing a stranger's dress.

"Here's the scoop. I love my music career so much, and I am so grateful—"

"Are you dodging the question, Ms. Rose?"

The premature interruption surprised her. "Not at all."

A deadly pause drifted over the airwaves.

"May I continue?" Mindy asked with attitude. She wasn't smiling now and was fine if the listeners knew that.

"Please. We do want to know. But we only have a twenty-minute spot." She let out a shrill laugh. No one else in the studio so much as chuckled, and Mindy was confident none of the listeners had either. She sneaked a look at Vern; it said, *I might walk out of here if she keeps it up.* She turned back to the microphone. "As I was saying, I am so grateful that I get to make music like I do and that I get to travel and meet so many awesome people who love music as much as I do."

Christy's expression grew more pinched with every word.

"I love music, and I love the people that music connects me to, and it is that love that motivates me to be completely honest here."

Finally, Christy looked interested.

"Though this is fun, and though I wouldn't trade it for anything"—Dustin's face popped into her mind. Was this still true? Maybe she would trade all her success for something else. The missing him came over her so powerfully then that she almost lost her train of thought. "And though I wouldn't trade it, it is true that it is incredibly fast paced. It takes a lot of energy. If someone pays for a ticket, travels to a show, and then waits for me to come on stage, I don't want to only half show up for that person. I want to give them my all. And so I've been pushing myself." She glanced at Vern, who was watching her carefully. "I pushed and pushed to give everyone everything I've got, so that meant that I wasn't getting enough rest or sleep, and I was getting way too much caffeine." She forced a laugh, though it wasn't funny.

"Are you saying that you ran off stage because you were *tired*?"

Ugh. What was *wrong* with this woman? "Nope. Definitely didn't say that." She completely failed to keep the tension out of her voice. "I was about to say that I was exhausted and overwhelmed, and I had a good old-fashioned panic attack."

"A panic attack?"

"That's exactly right." She worked hard not to be embarrassed. "It happens to the best of us. I couldn't breathe. I ran off stage. I put myself in a time out, and I'm feeling much better now. And we are taking steps—"

"So you're saying it had nothing to do with your lover in South Dakota?"

"I don't have a lover in South Dakota!" she snapped. "What is wrong with you?" Vern started to step in, but Mindy stood and held a hand up to stop him. "My story could actually help someone, and you're trying to pervert the truth. You should be ashamed of yourself." She forced herself to calm down. "To the listeners, I'm sorry to end this interview, but I'm doing so because I'm making my mental health a priority. I hope to see you at the show." She ripped the headphones off and dropped them on the table.

The red on-air sign blinked off. "No really, what is wrong with you?" Mindy took pleasure in the fact that the awful woman did now look embarrassed. Maybe even scared. Vern was ushering Mindy out of the studio, but she shook him off to thank the people behind the glass. She found the amused looks on their faces rather gratifying.

On their way down the stairs, one of her people said, "Anyone want to bet on her getting fired?"

"I hope not," Mindy said.

"Seriously? That seemed to be your intention a minute ago."

"I'm hoping she was having a bad day. And no, that was never my intention. But she was trying to spread lies about me. How was I supposed to react?"

"I think you did just fine," Vern said. "You are certainly keeping people guessing lately." He paused before opening the outside door. "We don't have time for photos this time."

"Yes we do," Mindy said. "We just left early." She pushed her way outside and smiled at the first person in line. She didn't know where this new boldness was coming from, but she rather liked it.

Chapter 42

Burke Honeywood was watching television while his wife Ava played on her phone beside him. His back was killing him, and he kept fidgeting. He knew he wouldn't find a position that was comfortable, but he wished he could find one that was less uncomfortable.

"Stop squirming," she said without looking up. "Can't you ever sit still?" She gasped.

He looked at her, waiting for an explanation.

She looked up, her eyes wide. "Uh, you might want to call Dustin."

"Why?" He tried to look at her phone, but the print was too tiny.

"Does he actually think he's like, in a relationship with that woman?"

"What?" Burke was annoyed. She was making his brother sound delusional. "I don't think he's planning on marrying her or anything. Why, what happened? Is she already hooking up with someone else?"

Finally, Ava handed him the phone.

Oh boy. "What website is this?"

"I don't know. I clicked on a link."

"Well it's probably like a tabloid or something. It's probably not true."

"But what if it is?"

He handed the phone back to her. "I'm not calling my brother to tell him about some gossip column." He turned back to the TV. He liked talking to Ava, but he wasn't enjoying this particular conversation.

"I think you should warn him, Burke, so he doesn't embarrass himself."

"What's he going to do, change his Facebook status to in-a-relationship?"

Ava punched him playfully. "Of course not. Fine. I'll call him." She acted like she was going to dial, and he put a hand over her phone.

"Please don't." He tried to think of a way to distract her. "Hey, let's order a pizza."

"Don't try to redirect me. And yes, a pizza would be great. But first, you need to call your brother. Come on, if it were you, you would want to know."

He raised his eyebrows. "I would want to know if you went on the radio and said you weren't dating anyone?"

She giggled. "Please, Burke? I'm not going to stop until you do."

He groaned. "Can I just text him?"

"I guess." She sounded disappointed.

He picked up his phone. "Send me the link—" He barely got the words out before his phone beeped with her message, which he copied and pasted into a message for Dustin. "Not to be a pot stirrer," he typed, "but ..." He didn't know how to finish that sentence, so he erased it and wrote, "Ava is making me send this. Sorry." Then he hurriedly hit send before she could edit him. He shoved the phone under his leg and rocked onto his left hip. This hurt a lot, but it gave his right hip a break. "So, let's order that pizza."

She sighed. "I know I said it sounded good, but we really don't have the funds. How about I make us a pizza?"

He felt bad for suggesting something that they couldn't afford. He felt bad for not winning any money in Missouri. "Sure, honey." He leaned over and gave her a quick peck. "Thank you."

Chapter 43

Dustin had just hit the South Dakota state line and pulled over for a pit stop when he saw Burke's message. He clicked on the link and then reread the headline three times before admitting to himself that it read what he'd thought it read the first time: "Mindy Rose Squashes Rumor of Deadwood Love Interest"

Feeling sick, he started reading, impatiently scrolling through the giant flashing ads that popped up after every two lines of text. The article, if he could even call it that, used lots of words to provide very little information, but what he gleaned was: Mindy had gone on country radio and emphatically told the world that she did *not* have a boyfriend in South Dakota. He might have been able to live with that, but the article also said that she'd called the radio host a pervert and snapped, "What is wrong with you?" for even suggesting such a thing.

He dropped his phone without answering Burke.

Fine. It was all fine. He shouldn't be upset. On some level he'd known this was coming. Well, maybe not something quite so rude and dismissive, but something similar. He'd known that she would forget all about him. Maybe she'd never liked him at all. Maybe she'd just used him to give herself a little vacation. But then he remembered that kiss in the fake loft—that kiss had *not* been faked. No one was that good of a faker.

He shook his head. He didn't want to think about it anymore. Figuring it out wouldn't do him any good. There was nothing to figure out. Whether she liked him or not, she was gone.

Long gone.

And he was going to go back to his life, a life that he'd loved back before he'd met Mindy Rose.

An hour later when he stopped for a snack, Dustin answered Burke so that Ava wouldn't worry about him. "Yeah," he texted, "I'm not surprised. No big deal." He hit send and then worried that he hadn't said enough. Ava might still read into that and think he wasn't okay. She'd be right, but he wanted to avoid that. "It was fun to hang out with her," he wrote, "but it was just fun, and I knew that. Thanks for your concern. But I'm really okay." He hit send and then went into the store intent on buying a big bag of greasy comfort food.

Chapter 44

3 Weeks Later

Mindy was finally going to get a break in her tour schedule. She had a whole week off. She was heading home to Alabama, finally, but she also wanted to go to South Dakota.

There was one small problem with this desire.

Dustin was ghosting her.

She didn't see how this was possible. He was such a nice guy that she really couldn't imagine him dodging her calls. But she also couldn't come up with another reason that she couldn't get in touch with him. She'd called, she'd left voice mails, she'd texted—she'd even messaged through social media. But nothing.

But as her short break grew closer, she knew she had to make a decision. Her last show was in Detroit. Then she had to either fly west or fly south. She called Keely for advice.

"Where are you?"

It took Mindy a few seconds to remember. "Austin. No, Houston. No, wait. Austin."

"Might want to find out for sure before you step out on stage and say, 'Hello, Dallas!'"

Mindy laughed. "I don't greet geographical locations for exactly that reason." She looked out her hotel window for some clue to confirm that she was in fact in Austin, but she didn't see any landmarks.

Mindy explained her dilemma to Keely and asked for advice.

"Don't you have someone there who could do some spying for you? I mean, I would do it, but you know, it's kind of a long drive, and I don't have a great track record for completing it."

Mindy laughed. "I don't have any spies."

"You had to have made a friend while you were there. You know, other than him."

She thought of Chase and laughed. "I don't know if I made *any* friends while I was there, and that's counting him." She sighed. "But you're right in that I was certainly friend*ly* with other people. The trouble is, they are all his family. I can't call one of his brothers up and ask him to spy."

"They were all brothers? He doesn't have a sister?"

"He does not." She thought of Olivia and gasped.

"What? You just thought of something."

"Maybe. I hardly know her, but man, she was so nice. I just have a feeling she would be nice about it if I called. She might not spy for me, but she wouldn't hang up on me either. I think."

"Okay, can I be blunt?"

"Since when did you ask permission first?"

"Touché. Okay. You need to call her. Because you need to figure this out. You are twenty-five years old, rich, and gorgeous. You need to be dating. If this guy isn't going to work out, then you need to find that out now so that you can start finding someone better."

Mindy was pretty sure there wasn't someone better in the whole wide world, but she got Keely's point. "Okay."

"Yeah?"

"Yeah." She groaned. "How the heck am I supposed to get a hold of her? I don't even know her last name."

"Well, who is she?"

"She's his brother Wyatt's girlfriend."

"So look Wyatt up online. He's probably tagged her in some photos."

"I don't think any of the Honeywood brothers are big on social media."

"No wonder their ranch is failing."

"It's not *failing*," she snapped. She tipped her head back and took a breath. She didn't need to be jumping to defend a ranch she had no connection with. "It's just on pause or something. Anyway ..."

"Where does she work?"

"I don't know." Inspiration struck. "The library! She works at the West Hope library!"

"Well, there you go."

"Okay, hanging up on you now to call the library before I lose my nerve."

"Okay. Call me back after, sista." Keely hung up.

Mindy searched for the number and dialed, hoping they were open and hoping Olivia was working.

"West Hope Library."

"Hi, Olivia?" She squeezed her eyes shut and braced herself.

"Uh, no."

"Oh, I'm sorry. May I please speak to Olivia?"

"Uh, no. She's not here. Who is this?"

Mindy wanted to cry. "I'm sorry. This is her friend. I just needed to talk to her, and I ... I can't seem to find her number."

The woman didn't say anything for several seconds. "I could pass on a message for you?"

"Oh yes, please. That would be so great. Can you just ask her to call Mindy? It's important." She rattled off her phone number.

"Mindy?" the woman repeated, and Mindy braced herself for the recognition. "Okay, Mindy, I'll let her know. Have a great day."

Mindy hung up and stared at the phone. But this was silly. That woman wasn't going to deliver the message right away, and even if she did, Olivia wasn't going to call her right away, *if* she even called her at all.

Mindy lay down and turned on the TV. She had about an hour before she had to start getting ready for tonight's show. With her luck, Olivia would call her just as she was stepping out on stage. She imagined herself holding up a hand to the crowd and saying, "Would you excuse me for a sec? I need to take this." Mindy finished her episode, started another one, and then came to terms with the fact that she wasn't going to hear from Olivia till after the show, if at all.

She got up and turned the shower on, feeling like she was moving in slow motion. She pressed play on her playlist and then climbed into the steam, and the water did perk her up a little, even if it was against her will. She had just lathered the shampoo through her hair when her phone rang. She jumped, grabbed it with one slippery hand, dropped it, shrieked, bent over to pick it up, and then stood up so fast she got dizzy. "Hello!" she nearly shouted into the phone. She gripped it so tightly that it started to squirt out of her hand, and she slapped her second hand over it, making a loud *splat* sound. "Hello?" she said again.

"Are you in the shower?"

"Olivia!" She turned the water off. "Hang on!" She searched for a towel, found one, and dried off the phone. "Hello? Thank you so much for calling me back." She put the phone on speaker and set it on the counter before she could bobble it again.

"Yeah, of course. Are you okay?"

"Yeah, I'm fine. Why?" All the phone juggling had left her panting.

"I don't know. The whole thing is just so mysterious. And then you called, so I thought maybe something was wrong."

"The whole *what* thing is so mysterious?"

"Oh nothing. It's none of my business. So what can I do for you?"

Mindy hardly knew this woman. She couldn't go making demands. She tried to calm her emotions. "I can't get a hold of Dustin, and I think he might be dodging my calls. I don't want to be all dramatic, but I was hoping maybe you could shed some light on the situation."

Olivia didn't say anything at first.

Mindy tried to be patient.

"Uh, he read about what you said about him on the radio."

"What? I didn't say anything about him on the ..." Her voice trailed off as she remembered. "Wait, Olivia, I really didn't say anything bad, but how did he read about that?"

"I don't know. It was online I guess."

Of course it was. "Olivia, I didn't say anything bad." *You already told her that.* "I got annoyed because they used the word lover. I said I didn't have a *lover*. I didn't say anything about him specifically. Certainly nothing bad."

She sucked in some air. "Oh boy."

"Yeah. What is going on? Does he hate me?"

"No, more like he's crushed. But don't say that I said that. He won't actually say a word about it. If someone brings you up, he leaves the room."

"Oh no." Mindy carefully picked the phone up and carried it to the bed. "Olivia, I like him a lot." *Liked* wasn't the right word, but she stuck with it. "And I finally have a chance to come see him. But I need to ask him if he even wants that? I guess?" She felt sick. For three weeks he'd thought she'd dissed him. Three weeks?

"Ah, he wants you to. Just come. I'll pick you up at the airport."

"Seriously?"

"Yeah, of course."

"Olivia, you're the best! I don't know how to thank you."

"Oh, don't you worry. I've got a big favor to ask of you."

"What?"

She laughed. "I'll tell you when I see you. I'm calling you now from my cell, so you have my number now. You can call or text me your flight info?"

"Sure. Will do. Are you going to tell them that I'm coming?"

"Do you want me to?"

"I don't know."

"I won't tell them unless you tell me to. I happen to know that the Honeywoods love surprises."

Chapter 45

"How was your date?"

Dustin grimaced. "It was okay." He couldn't really complain. He'd practically begged his coworker to set him up with his sister, and the guy had finally done it.

"I tried to warn you."

"Yeah, yeah."

"She's all about you, though." He whistled. "Thinks you're the cat's meow."

Dustin felt ill. "I'm really not."

"Well." He slapped Dustin on the back. "Let her down gently, will ya?" He sauntered off.

Dustin had already let her down gently. Now he was going to have to change his number. As if beckoned by his bad mood, his phone rang. He barked his hello and then felt guilty when it was Olivia. "Oh, hey, Olivia, sorry."

"Having a bad day?"

"Yeah"—he glanced at the clock—"but it's almost over."

"Oh goodie."

Goodie? "Why, what's up?"

"Can you come out to the ranch?"

"I'm pretty tired." And he didn't want to be around people. Like ever again. He had thought that dating other women would help, but he'd been on three dates in three weeks, and each of them had progressively gotten worse. He was done. Done with humanity.

"Please? I have an idea for how to make Hudson's plan work."

"Hudson's plan? Wasn't this originally your plan?"

"My idea. But Hudson's plan. And now I have another idea."

"I admire your enthusiasm." Though he wasn't in the mood for it, he did admire it. "But that really has nothing to do with me. You're a little far from town water pipes."

She laughed as if he'd said something hysterical. How charitable of her. "Oh, it very much has to do with you. In fact, you're the linchpin."

The *linchpin*? How could he possibly be the linchpin? "That's kind of you to say, but I'm going to have to pass. Maybe some other—"

"Dustin." Her tone had changed so drastically that she sounded like someone else. "Please. I really need you there. Do it for Chase."

He wanted to reach through the phone and smack her. She knew that he wouldn't say no to Chase, and that was so manipulative of her. He'd never been mad at Olivia, but he was now. Fine. He would go to whatever this was, and then they would all regret that she'd invited him. "What time?" he said through a clenched jaw.

"We're here now. Come as soon as you can."

"We? Who's we?"

She hesitated. "You know, the regulars." Her voice was suspicious.

"No, Olivia. I don't know. Who's there?" And was it too late for him to back out?

"You'll see when you get here. I've got to stir before I burn supper. See you soon!"

He stared at the phone, unbelieving that she'd used stirring as an excuse. She had called him from a cell phone, for crying out loud. She could have just carried it to the stove with her.

Dustin waited for the clock to run out and then pointed his truck toward the ranch. At least he was going to get some Olivia-food out of this. It wouldn't solve all of his problems. It wouldn't even solve one of his problems. But it would sure taste good.

You only have one problem, an annoying voice in his head told him.

True, and he had to get over it. He was furious with himself that it still hurt. He wished he'd never met Mindy Rose. She could have stayed one of those mythical creatures in the TV.

When he arrived at the ranch, he eyed the vehicles suspiciously, but he didn't see anyone unusual. Olivia's new car and Hudson's truck were out front, and he figured Chase's truck was parked in the back. Feeling relieved, he got out of the truck and went inside.

No one greeted him when he walked in, and he looked up to see why everyone was so quiet.

And that's when he saw her.

His mouth fell open, and he couldn't quite pull it shut again.

She smiled so brilliantly, as if she was so happy to see him, as if she'd never publicly insulted him. She came toward him slowly as if she were afraid he was going to run away. Then she tentatively put her arms around him before pulling him in for a tight hug. He tried to stop himself from melting into her, but he failed. "We need to talk," she whispered into his ear.

Yeah, no kidding.

"Mindy just got here," Hudson said. "You should take her out and show her Chase's new horse."

Nice try, Hudson. Chase hasn't gotten a new horse in months.

Mindy clutched his arm. "Oh, yes, please. I would love to see the horses."

Speechless, Dustin went back outside. They'd barely cleared the porch before she spun on him. "Okay, I'm madly in love with you, and I'm really sorry that you read some baloney article that misquoted me, but we both could have avoided a lot of angst if you would just *pick up your phone.*" Her voice got louder—and noticeably less affectionate—with each word.

Dustin didn't know whether to laugh or cry. After a long, stupid hesitation, he managed, "What?"

Mindy glared at him. "I have been *worried*, Dustin. Actually worried! I searched your name online because I thought that you must have been in a horrible accident because that is the only reason I could come up with that you would be *dodging my calls!*" She hit him in the shoulder. "You dodged my calls! You're a jerk!"

Because he was in something like a state of shock, and because he didn't know which emotion to feel, or how to react, he laughed.

Her eyes grew wide. She was taking his laugh as a challenge.

He rubbed his arm. "You hit me!"

She laughed too then. "Stop! It's not funny! I'm mad at you!"

This reminded him that he too was mad. Why he couldn't *feel* that anger was another story, but he needed to be mad. He had good reason. "Mindy, you went on the *air* and said I didn't exist! How did you think I was going to react to that—"

"I said no such thing! I was misquoted, taken out of context, and more. But even if I *did* say that, you don't just ghost me, Dustin! Why wouldn't you call me and talk it out? Even if we argue, even if we break up, at least then we'd know where we stand!"

Wait, *what?* "Break up?"

"I don't want to break up!" she cried. "Do you?"

Chapter 46

How could a man this smart possibly be this stupid? Mindy stared at Dustin, waiting for him to answer her question. She hadn't realized a yes-or-no question could be so complicated.

"Break up," he repeated.

She waited for him to say something sensible.

"We'd have to be a couple before we could break up," he said slowly.

"Uh ... okay." Wow, maybe she'd been wrong about him. Had he bumped his head on the way home from Reno or something?

"I thought ..." he started.

"What? What did you think?"

"I thought that you didn't ..."

The door opened behind them, and Wyatt stuck his head out. "Uh, the horses are out back."

"Go away, Wyatt," Dustin said.

Wyatt gave him a dirty look. "Olivia asked me to tell you that food will be ready in five."

"Thank you," Mindy said. She waited for the door to close and then looked at Dustin. "Will you please talk to me?" The ground beneath her started to feel shaky. "This can't work if you won't talk to me."

"I'm so sorry." He looked at the ground. "The truth is ... I was starting to have doubts, and then when I saw that article, it just confirmed what I already thought I knew." He picked his head up, and his eyes met hers. "What are you doing here?"

She shrugged. "You wouldn't answer your phone. I had to know where I stood." She wanted to go to him again, to bury her face in his neck, to feel his arms around her, but she wasn't going to beg. The ball was in his court.

"What do you want?" he asked.

"What do I want?" Hadn't she already made that clear enough? "I want *you*!"

That did it. He closed the gap between them and took her into his arms and kissed her firmly. As the kiss lengthened, it softened, and his tenderness made her dizzy. She dug her fingers into his shirt to keep herself from falling.

The door opened again, and Wyatt laughed. "Uh, supper."

Mindy pulled away and looked up into Dustin's eyes.

"That was a quick five minutes," Dustin said.

She didn't argue, but she thought that kiss had probably lasted longer than he'd thought it had. "Time is funny when you're in love."

He nodded. "Yes, yes, it is. This has been the longest, most awful three weeks of my life."

"Me too."

He ran his hand down her arm and took her hand into his. "We should go eat."

"Okay, but hey." She waited for him to look at her. "I didn't say any of those things."

He nodded. "I'm sorry that I believed it."

"Trust me, Dustin. You're going to hear things because people lie. But you know me. I'm the same weird girl you found stowing away in the back of your truck."

He laughed. "Okay."

"Okay, let's go eat." On their way up the steps, she said, "Oh, and they said I could cut our song on the next album."

"What?" he cried. "That's incredible."

She giggled. "I thought you'd like that."

Hudson looked up. "Wow, you're happy."

Dustin gave him the songwriting news, and they all congratulated him as they settled around the table.

After Hudson said grace, Olivia cleared her throat. "I have an idea."

Wyatt moaned, and Chase looked nervous.

Neither reaction slowed Olivia down. "I know that we've been having trouble booking people for the event center."

Chase closed his eyes. He appeared to be meditating. Mindy realized that she'd missed Chase, and she found that a little weird.

"We need to have a grand opening!" Olivia waited for a reaction that did not come. She swept her arm toward Mindy. "And we have our opening act! I mean, you're not the opening act. You're the act for the opening. I know you're not an opening act anymore. I'm sorry—"

"I knew what you meant," Mindy said quickly, squeezing Dustin's hand, "and I would love to do a show here for you. But I told Olivia that I have conditions."

Chase groaned.

"And what might those be?" Hudson pushed his glasses up and stared at her, intrigued.

"First, the attendance could get out of hand so quickly. You're going to have to figure out a way to limit it. Invitation only or something. You'll need security. And don't try to keep it a secret. That has a very good chance of failing."

"We couldn't even keep you a secret when we didn't know who you were," Hudson said.

She sneaked a look at Dustin. He had known. He'd known all along. But he hadn't really cared much.

"And how many other conditions are there?" Chase said.

"Just one." She took a deep breath. She knew this part might make her sound a bit loony. "I want to find the woman who gave me her dress, and I want her in the front row."

"What?" Dustin said. "How are we supposed to do that?"

"I can post it on my social media, promising tickets to her and to whomever helps me find her."

"Uh ... Mindy?" Dustin sounded like he was about to burst her bubble.

She looked at him expectantly.

"What if that woman isn't your fan? I mean, she wasn't even at your show."

Mindy chuckled. She'd already thought of that. "I know. But I still think she might enjoy an all-expense paid trip to a swanky event center for a free concert."

Wyatt snorted. "Swanky."

"Okay, maybe not swanky, but you know what I mean. *Nice.*"

"What if thousands of people claim to be your dress woman?" Hudson asked.

"I don't think that will happen, but if it does, I'll ask them to send a picture. I'll recognize her." That woman's face was one of the few things she remembered from that awful night.

Chase shook his head. "Watch her be from Australia or something."

"Australia?" Wyatt cried.

"People come from all over for Wild Bill Days."

"I don't think they come from Australia!" As far as Wyatt was concerned, Australia might be on the moon.

No one said anything for several seconds.

Olivia broke the silence with clapping. "Isn't this a great plan?"

Mindy didn't know if it even qualified as a plan yet, but either way, she was excited about it. Maybe not as excited as Olivia, but excited.

Chapter 47

D ustin wasn't a big fan of flying, but his work schedule did not afford him the time to drive to and from Alabama, no matter how much he enjoyed road tripping with Mindy. They arrived at the airport ridiculously early, and he followed Mindy's instructions to park in the parking lot like a normal person.

As soon as he pulled his nose into the spot, a black limo pulled in behind him. It took a few seconds to register that it was there for them. "What's going on?"

She smiled mischievously. "They're going to take us to the plane."

"What?"

A man in a suit took their luggage while a woman in a TSA uniform waved a wand up and down each side of them. Then she went and checked their luggage while the man in the suit opened the back door for them. Mindy comfortably thanked him and then slid into the car first. Wondering if he was supposed to tip, Dustin got in and settled in beside her. "So you're used to all this, huh?"

"Used to what, limos?"

"To being rich in general."

She didn't answer him.

"Are we supposed to tip him?"

"I'll take care of it."

He tried not to let this insult his manhood. He was out of his element, for sure, but he was working to be okay with that. "Okay, but why are we in a limousine?"

She giggled. "This protects me from signing autographs in front of our gate. Not that I mind. I don't. But the airport minds. It creates a human dam."

Apparently their luggage passed inspection because the TSA agent climbed into the front, and then they were off. He still didn't understand where they were going exactly. How was this limo going to get them onto the plane? Didn't they have to walk through that big shaky tube thing?

But he soon figured it out, and then he felt stupid. They walked up a small set of portable stairs and into the end of the tube, where they were warmly greeted by a flight attendant and shown to first class. They settled in and said no thank you to the drink offers. He buckled up. He really didn't like planes. He turned and looked over his shoulder.

"We're the only ones here, but soon they will all walk by and stare."

"Is that why you wanted the window seat?"

"No, I wanted the window seat so I could see out the window." She pulled some sunglasses out of her purse. "These are to cut down on the staring."

He chuckled. He hadn't fought for the window seat because he wasn't sure he wouldn't need to jump up and run to the tiny bathroom to throw up.

She reached over the pesky armrest and rubbed his leg. "Are you okay? Want me to find you some sleeping pills?"

He laughed. He didn't want to know how she planned on doing that. He put his hand over hers. "No, if I only get you for one week, I want to be awake as much as possible." He sighed. "Even if I have to do it thirty thousand feet in the air."

She laughed. "It'll be worth it. You're going to get to see the great state of Alabama. Best state in the union." She winked.

He rolled his eyes. "We can agree to disagree on that."

They had two layovers, one in Minneapolis and one in Atlanta, which they spent in a second and third limo. When they stepped off the plane in Mobile, Alabama, he was relieved to see an ordinary van was picking them up. "What, no limos in Bama?" he joked.

"They try to keep me humble."

He didn't think they would have to work very hard at that.

The van took them to a remote parking lot, where she'd secretly arranged to meet Keely.

Finally, he found out that Keely was indeed a real person. She jumped out of her car, ran to them, and flung her arms around Mindy. She held her, rocking her back and forth with an excitement he found bizarre.

Then she looked at him. "Wow, sista. You weren't kiddin'. He's a looker." And then that bizarreness was on him, and she was trying to rock his body left and right as Mindy looked on, laughing.

"Come on, you goofball, before we get caught."

Dustin was relegated to the back seat as Mindy and Keely sat up front talking a mile a minute. Like some kind of magic trick, Mindy's already significant southern accent doubled in strength. He missed at least ten percent of what she said now—maybe more. So he admired the scenery, which, he didn't want to admit, was pretty cool. He hadn't been prepared for the palm trees and they made the location feel exotic.

As they headed out of the city and into the country, he relaxed and really began to enjoy the view. The roads narrowed, and the forest grew thicker, closer, and greener. The trees spread their limbs out over the road creating a canopy, so it was like driving through a green tunnel—a tunnel of life, he thought. *Hey, that's pretty clever.* He made a quick note in his phone. If he and Mindy ever tried to write another song, maybe they could use that.

He was almost sad to enter the next town but soon abandoned that sadness. This small village was so spread out that it still felt like country—one house per block with giant sprawling green lawns. He had no desire to leave South Dakota, but he could see why Mindy loved her home state.

Keely pulled into a long driveway, each side of which was lined with large, shapely rose bushes in full pink bloom. He could smell them through the windows. "What is this, the botanical gardens?"

Mindy giggled. "No, this is Mom's place." As she said it, the giant sweeping mansion came into view, and he nearly gasped.

"Holy smokes," he managed.

"Yeah."

"No wonder you need to make money."

She laughed again. "Yeah. But she's worth every penny."

A few people stared as they went in the front door, and one woman ran up to ask for an autograph, but most of the people acted like Mindy Rose was no big deal. Like she owned the place, Mindy led them down a long hallway with a high ceiling. She stopped in front of a door with a sign that read, "Mrs. Katherine Rose." She knocked on the door, and it soon opened.

"Oh, you don't have to knock dear." Mrs. Rose stepped back to let them in, and Dustin couldn't believe how nervous he was. He felt like he was meeting the President.

She hugged her daughter, hugged Keely and called her by name, then straightened as much as she could while still leaning on her cane, and looked at Dustin. "And you must be him."

Dustin laughed. "I hope so."

Her eyes lit up, and in that moment, she looked just like Mindy. "Great answer, my boy!" She hugged him with a strength that surprised him and then let go to say, "Y'all sit down! You must be worn slap out!"

He didn't know what that meant, but he assumed he was supposed to sit beside Mindy, so he did, and Keely sat on the other side of him, so he felt like the good part of a sandwich.

"So, how are you feeling, Mom?"

"Oh, fine as a frog's hair!"

Dustin laughed, and Mindy gave him a confused look. He tried to apologize with his eyes as he wondered how that *wasn't* funny.

Mom and daughter talked for a while, as he and Keely listened. He was happy to be left out of it and was enjoying being the audience. He couldn't believe how much these two women were alike. But then, all of a sudden, Mrs. Rose abruptly launched a fusillade of questions at him: Ever been married? Any kids? What did his parents do? Oh, she was so sorry to hear they'd passed. Where did he work? Go to school? Did he like his job? Opportunity for advancement? She stopped just shy of asking him how much money he made, but he told her anyway.

"Mom, that's enough," Mindy said once he'd started to sweat.

Mrs. Rose narrowed her eyes and smiled. "You're going to have to work pretty hard to keep up with my daughter."

"I've noticed."

Her smile widened. "She's worth it."

He nodded, knowing that a new gravity had been added to the conversation. "I know that."

"So you'll take good care of her." It was more of an order than a question.

"Yes, ma'am. I sure will."

Chapter 48

M indy had put her publicist to good use. They'd capped the attendance at three hundred, invited every wedding planner, dress shop owner, florist, and baker within two hundred miles, and then had a free lottery pick for the rest of the tickets.

But the two seats front and center were still reserved.

Mindy had posted on all of her social media profiles, asking for the mystery woman to come forward so that she could thank her, but she'd only heard from imposters, and the event was tomorrow. She was starting to think that her plan wasn't going to work, that she was never going to be able to return the dress, never going to be able to hug this woman and tell her how much she'd helped her—how she'd changed the entire course of her life.

The barn looked amazing. Olivia and Wyatt had really outdone themselves. Lights hung from strings draped from the beams. Swathes of white silk hung from the walls. Hay was scattered on the floor so unevenly Mindy knew it had taken great care and effort. And the barn now had a stage. Not too high, but it would be perfect for a bride and groom to stand on as they said their vows.

Everyone would be able to see.

She looked up at the fake hayloft, where two bales of real hay now sat. She knew how they'd gotten there, the secret entrance they'd used.

Her phone beeped, and she ignored it. It had been going off constantly since she'd opened up her private messages so that dress woman could get in touch with her.

So it wasn't until hours later, when she was snuggled up on the couch at Dustin's house that she forced herself to get caught up on the messages.

"What is it?" Dustin asked.

She looked up. "How did you know it was anything?"

"You stopped breathing."

She smiled. She hoped he always paid that much attention to her. "This girl messaged me, sent me a picture of her mother, and said she's too shy to reach out." She held up her phone. "That's her."

"Where does she live?"

She checked the girl's profile. "She lives in Spearfish."

"Seriously?"

"Is that close?"

"In South Dakota miles, it's very close. Hey, you should screenshot that and send it to Olivia. Maybe she knows her."

"Why would Olivia know her?"

"Olivia is from Spearfish." He said this as if she were stupid.

She rolled her eyes. "How was I supposed to know that?"

"Mindy, you need to focus and apply yourself if you're going to learn everything about the Honeywoods."

She laughed and hit him with a pillow. Then she sent the picture to Olivia with a question, "Do you know this woman?" Her phone rang, and Mindy groaned. "Now look what you did." She tried to sound friendly when she answered.

"That's Hannah McDaniel!"

"Okay. Who's Hannah McDaniel?"

"She is well, she's kind of a nut. But she's awesome! We used to go to the same church."

"Told you so," Dustin said, his mouth full of Doritos.

"Well, it's her. She's the dress lady."

"Oh my word, you're kidding. Of course she is. She is so nice and so helpful. When I was in ... I think it was seventh grade, I was getting picked on, and she somehow knew it. She found me hiding in the side room and helped me sneak out of the church to get away from the kids. Then she sat at the picnic table so I wouldn't be outside alone. She didn't say much, but I've always wondered how she knew what was going on."

"The evidence suggests she is pretty intuitive."

"I'll say. Okay, so she messaged you? Is she coming?"

"She did not. Her daughter did."

"Oh, April!"

"Yeah. She said her mother is too shy to come forward."

She laughed. "She's not shy. She's just humble. Probably doesn't want to be thanked. But you should go to her. Want me to show you where she lives?"

Mindy laughed. "I can't just show up at her house."

Dustin looked at his phone. "You could be there by seven."

"Didn't you have something planned for the concert?" Olivia asked.

"Not really. I have a card, and I was going to give her a good show, though I'm starting to think she really isn't a fan."

"She might not be. She seems the type to only listen to Jesus-tunes."

"She was at a *bar* when I found her."

"At an outdoor bar, though, right? Who knew what she was doing. Anyway, you're at Dustin's? I'll be right there." Olivia hung up.

Dustin eyed her. "Do you want me to go with you?"

She nodded. "I don't want to go at all. But yes."

He patted her leg. "It'll be great."

Thirty minutes later, Olivia was driving them to a town called Spearfish.

"It's an odd name for a town, Spearfish."

"Apparently the American Indians used to spear fish in the creek there," Olivia said. "Spearfish Creek."

"That makes sense. Guess it's not that odd of a name, then."

"It's an odd creek, though. Freezes from the bottom up."

Mindy laughed. "What?"

"No, it's true," she insisted. "The water moves so fast that it can't freeze on the top, but it freezes on the bottom, so you can fish it year-round."

Mindy didn't understand the physics of this, but she didn't need to.

"Ugh," Olivia said when they hit the town line. "It's a great town, but I sure do have some baggage here."

"I'm sorry," Mindy said. Dustin had told her about what Olivia had been through.

"No need to be. It all led me to where I am now, which is a very, very good place." She signaled and turned right. "I sure do hope she hasn't moved. It's been a while."

Yeah, Mindy hoped she hadn't moved either, since they'd just driven to Spearfish. "I can't believe we're just going to show up. It feels rude. What if she's in her pajamas?"

"Maybe she'll rip them off and give them to you," Dustin said from the back seat.

Mindy didn't want to laugh at that, but she couldn't stop herself.

"If we warned her that we were coming, she might have run off and hid," Olivia said. "We're not going to push our way in or anything. You just thank her and then get back in the car."

Mindy found her phrasing alarming. "You're not coming with me?"

"Naw. I've got to keep the getaway car idling out front." She laughed at her own joke.

Mindy turned around and looked at Dustin. "You're coming, right?"

"Of course, my dear." He didn't sound thrilled.

Mindy was unreasonably nervous when she knocked on the door, and it felt like forever before it swung open. The lovely woman on the other side of it, the heroic Hannah McDaniel, gave her a wry look. "So you found me."

Mindy opened her mouth to say something charming, but instead, she burst into tears.

"Oh, sweetheart, get in here." Hannah pulled her inside and wrapped her in a hug.

"Sorry, I didn't mean to get so emotional."

Hannah let go of her and stepped back. "It's all good. It happens to the best of us."

Mindy wiped her eyes and held out her hands. One held a card. The other held a plastic sack with a dress neatly folded in it. "Here is your dress back, freshly laundered, and here is a little thank you. It's not much, but I had to do something."

A bit grudgingly, Hannah took the envelope. "It was nothing. Really. But thank you." She opened the sack and peeked in at the dress. Then she laughed. "I guess I picked the right dress to wear that night. Easy off, easy on."

Mindy laughed through her tears. "I really loved that dress. You've got good taste."

Hannah held it out to her. "Do you want to keep it?"

Mindy pushed the bag away. "No, no. It's yours."

"I wasn't even supposed to be there, you know. My daughter called me for a ride. She'd had too much to drink. I was annoyed to be there, but then I saw you and knew that you needed some help." She shook her head. "I haven't told many lies in the last decade, but that was one of them. I pointed those men chasing you in the exact wrong direction, God forgive me."

Mindy reached out and squeezed her hand. "I think he's forgiven you. Hannah, you did more than just give me a dress. You changed my entire life that night just by helping. Thank you for listening to your intuition and for stepping in."

Hannah smiled. "You're welcome." She held up the card. "And thank you."

Mindy sighed. She'd done what she'd come to do. "Are you sure you don't want to come to the show in West Hope tomorrow? We've saved you a seat, front and center."

"No, thank you, but please don't be offended."

"Nope, I'm not," she said, though she kind of was. She hoped the woman couldn't intuit that as well. "But if you ever do want to catch a show, just let me know. I've got connections."

Hannah laughed. "I'll bet you do."

Mindy remembered that Dustin was there, lurking in the doorway. She took hold of his arm with both hands. "I'm leaving, I promise, but I just want you to meet Dustin. He's the man of my dreams, and I met him that night because of you."

Hannah beamed. "I've always had a knack for accidental match-making. Good to hear I've still got it."

Mindy laughed. "Okay, I'll get out of your hair. You have a good night, Hannah. It's so good to know you."

Hannah nodded. "Good to know you too. I'm glad it all worked out." She held the door open for her, and Mindy held onto Dustin all the way to the car, where he opened the door for her. She thanked him and sank into the front seat. She was exhausted.

As Olivia pulled away from the house, Hannah came out onto her porch, waving the card over her head.

"What's she saying?" Olivia asked in alarm.

"She's saying, 'It's too much,'" Dustin said.

Mindy smiled and leaned her head back. Mission accomplished.

"How much did you put in that card, Mindy?"

"Not nearly enough."

Mindy nearly dozed off on the ride back to West Hope and when she opened her eyes, she realized Olivia was taking her back to Dustin's house. "I'm sorry, I should have asked you sooner. Would you mind dropping me off at my hotel?"

"I can run you back later," Dustin said.

"Thank you, but if Olivia doesn't mind, I really need to get to bed. I'm stupid tired." Emotions wore her out.

"Sure. No problem." Olivia turned around and headed south.

When she pulled into the parking lot, Mindy felt bad. "And one more thing, would you mind waiting till Dustin walks me inside? Sorry, I didn't plan this very well, but I'm too tired to get mobbed, and it's less likely to happen if Dustin's there."

"No problem," Olivia said again. "Really, it's okay. I like being friends with a celebrity."

Mindy chuckled. Soon to be family, she hoped.

Dustin held her hand and walked her to the elevator. "Want me to ride up with you too?"

"If you wouldn't mind."

"Not at all. I love elevators."

She giggled. "Sure you do."

As the large silver doors slid shut behind them, Dustin said, "Okay, tell me how much was in that card."

She raised her eyebrows. "Are you managing my finances now?"

He laughed. "No, I am definitely not. I'm just wondering if you're as generous as I think you are."

She stepped to him and pressed her lips to his.

The elevator dinged, and the doors slid open.

He walked her to her door and kissed her again. "So you're not going to tell me?"

She thought about it. "Nah. It's important to keep a little mystery in the relationship."

He laughed and stepped back. "Okay." He shook his head. "Good night, Mindy Rose. I sure am madly in love with you."

"Right back at you, Dustin Honeywood. Right back at you."

Epilogue

Dustin stood against the barn wall and watched the crowd watch the stage. They had hired security, but all the Honeywood brothers were acting as if they were part of the team. They couldn't help it. This was Hudson and Chase's home. They needed to keep it safe.

But so far, the crowd was incredibly tame. They sat in their seats politely waiting for the house lights to dim. And when they did, a hush fell over them. The music started, and the stage lights came up, and then Mindy Rose—his Mindy Rose—stepped out onto the stage and belted out that first note—and it was a good thing he was leaning against a sturdy barn wall because she took his breath away.

Somehow this was the first time he'd seen her on stage in real life, up close. And no wonder she was famous. She was a legend. Her beauty, her charm, her voice hitting all the right notes.

Halfway through her first song, her eyes found him, and she smiled so brightly he could hardly stand it. He blew her a kiss, and she danced away singing a song she liked wearing an outfit she was comfortable in—which so happened to be designed by her new stylist, one Natalie Reynolds from Casper, Wyoming.

Dustin couldn't believe how well it had all worked out. He couldn't believe how happy he was. Somehow he'd ended up dating a country music superstar, and he couldn't wait to marry her.

"She sure is something," Hudson shouted.

Dustin jumped a little. He'd been so riveted, he hadn't realized he was standing right beside him. "She sure is," Dustin agreed.

"I wish she had a sister," he said loudly.

Dustin laughed. "I thought you were in love with that nurse!"

A woman seated nearby gave them a dirty look, and Dustin held up a hand to tell her he was sorry. Then he looked at Hudson and mimed zipping his lips shut. Hudson rolled his eyes and leaned against the wall to watch. Dustin looked across the barn and saw Wyatt standing in the shadows. Beside him, Olivia bounced up and down to the beat. Burke and Ava had seats near the front. Ava looked really excited to be there. And Seth stood in the back, near the door, between two bouncers they'd actually hired. Dustin scanned the barn to confirm that Chase was not there, but that was no surprise. He was likely out guarding the horses, and was likely very happy with that arrangement.

Dustin turned his attention to the stage and soaked it all up, not wanting to miss another note. Mindy finished her opening number, and the small crowd went wild. She waited for the roar to settle down and then introduced herself, welcomed them all to the Honeywood Ranch, and then congratulated the Honeywood Brothers on their grand opening. "And I'd like to thank them for letting me be part of the party! So let's get back to it. Should we do another song? Yeah? Y'all going to help me out? How about a love song?"

She smiled at him. "Yeah, let's do a love song!"

Yes, let's, Dustin thought. *Let's do a love song.*

www.ingramcontent.com/pod-product-compliance
Lightning Source LLC
Chambersburg PA
CBHW032216070925
32253CB00016B/152

lines were even worse—each of them made her progressively more nauseous:

"Mindy Rose Spotted in Deadwood Bar with Married Local." Oh, for heaven's sake.

"Mindy Rose Quits Tour to Elope with Drummer." This one almost made sense, as she and John were good friends. But he was already married.

"Mindy Rose Walks Off Stage over Costume Dispute." This one landed the closest to reality.

"Mindy Rose's New Meds Cause Breakdown." If she'd had new meds, she might have avoided the breakdown. *I didn't have a breakdown*, she reminded herself. She hadn't hallucinated or gotten violent.

And the award for worst headline of them all had to go to: "Mindy Rose's Young Career Is Dead in Deadwood." Her career wasn't even close to dead—especially if she got right back on the horse. Randy Travis, her personal hero, had passed out naked in the middle of the road. Fans, herself included, had gotten over that pretty quickly. Though wearing that stupid tube dress was a lot like being naked, and yes, she'd been in the middle of Main Street, but she hadn't passed out.

She hadn't broken any laws, cheated on her spouse, said something hateful, or kicked out any footlights.

She would be fine.

She knew this. And yet, the ridiculous headlines still stung, and she really wished she hadn't pressed *search*.